"Where do you think the line is, Gianna, between the police department's need to protect its investigation and the public's need for information to protect itself?" Mimi asked carefully.

"I didn't come here to argue semantics with you. I don't have time for that." Gianna's anger had not diminished.

"It's not semantics. It's a real issue. It's a real problem that the press and the police need to fix and I'd like to think that you and I can —"

Gianna cut her off with icy anger. "I asked you not to run a story."

"I don't work that way. I never have and I never will." Now Mimi was angry.

They stood facing each other, holding each other with their eyes for a long moment before Gianna spoke — softly but with traces of anger still lingering.

"If whatever we have between us is to survive this case —"

Mimi cut her off with razor-sharp swiftness. "Don't call it 'whatever,' Gianna. It has a name, what we have between us. Don't you know what it is? Or are you afraid to call it by that name?"

KEEPING SECRETS

A GIANNA MAGLIONE MYSTERY

PENNY MICKELBURY

The Naiad Press, Inc.
1994

Printed in the United States of America on acid-free paper
First Edition

Edited by Katherine V. Forrest
Cover design by Pat Tong and Bonnie Liss
  (Phoenix Graphics)
Typeset by Sandi Stancil

Library of Congress Cataloging-in-Publication Data

Mickelbury, Penny, 1948–
    Keeping secrets : a Gianna Maglione mystery / by Penny
Mickelbury.
        p.   cm.
    ISBN 1-56280-052-3
    1. Private investigators—Fiction.   2. Women detectives—Fiction.
3. Lesbians—Fiction.
PS3563.I3517K4   1994
813'.54—dc20   93-41787
                                                                CIP

Dedication

This work is dedicated with love to the memory of my brother, Crawford Oliver Mickelbury; and with gratitude to my good friend, Dianne, who challenged me to write this book.

About the Author

Penny Mickelbury was a newspaper, radio, and television reporter in Washington, D.C. for more than a decade. She also was the Assistant News Director at a Washington television station. She currently lives and writes in New York City.

I

"Aw, hell, not another one!"

The night security guard responsible for patrolling the exterior grounds and parking lots in the northeast quadrant of the Washington, D.C. public schools had already chased three cars of amorous teens from the dark corners of the mammoth George Washington High School lot. Sometimes he didn't mind because some of what he saw in the back seats of cars was better than the magazines he brought to keep himself amused between 10:00 p.m. and 3:00 a.m., the magic final

1

hour when some over-paid school system bureaucrat believed all mayhem directed at public school facilities would mysteriously cease. But tonight he'd had enough and that's just exactly what he'd tell the heavy breathers in that car back there. He checked his watch, idly wondering what time the car had arrived.

He'd left this lot at exactly 10:20 and made the rounds of the other six schools on his rotation rounds, activities which had included interrupting a drug deal on the steps of Roosevelt Elementary School; chasing — and almost catching — two eleven-year-olds who were spray-painting graffiti on the tennis courts at Carver Junior High; reporting a robbery in progress at the dental lab across the street from Girls High and waiting for the police to arrive; and stopping at the 7-Eleven for a cup of coffee. Here he was back at 12:30. He drove diagonally across the empty lot, thankful he didn't have the day shift when fifteen hundred cars and three times that many students would have made the job a misery. He pulled up perpendicular to a brand new white Lincoln Town Car and turned on his high beams. That usually got the kids' attention. No response. Feeling an odd unease, he grabbed his flashlight and got out.

He could see a figure sitting upright in the driver's seat. No teenage hanky-panky here. He sidled up to the car and shone his light inside. The man didn't move. He couldn't, and would never again. His hands were cupped in his lap, almost gracefully, covering what was left of the genitals that had been blown away by a very large gun. The guard wrote in his log book: *Mon. Oct. 21, 91,*

2

12:30am before he turned and threw up his supper. And as he retched he had the thought that maybe he should have written Tues. Oct. 22nd.

II

After eighteen years as a cop, the late night and early morning ringing of the telephone was a common if unwelcome occurrence, so the head of the Hate Crimes Unit of the Washington, D.C. police force easily awakened from a deep sleep on the second ring of her phone.

"Hello," she said, as clear-voiced as if it were noon.

"It's me, Anna. There's been another one, but you don't really need to come down here —"

"Thanks for the call, Eric. I'm on my way," she said, gently but firmly overriding his protestations.

She looked at the clock. Not quite one. She wrote down the address Eric gave her and was en route to the shower with the cellular phone when she said to him, "See you in thirty."

She stepped into the steaming water with an overwhelming sense of dread. If Eric was right, somebody in the Nation's capital had murdered four wealthy, professional gay people and no one had the slightest idea who or why. She knew only that the murders served as proof to the doubters that the newly-formed Hate Crimes Unit would pay for itself. The murders also had catapulted her out of her role as the administrator of the Hate Crimes Unit and into the fray as an investigator, a role she quite frankly preferred to and performed better than that of administrator.

In the one hundred and fifty seconds it took her to shower, she relived the year of persuading and arguing and arm-twisting required to convince the bureaucracy of the need for a special unit within the Department to investigate only those crimes committed against persons or groups based on their race, color, religion, or sexual preference. She'd lost the fight to include crimes against women in the mission statement, and in this moment, was grateful. She felt overwhelmed by the task before her; a bigger burden would have weighed much too heavily.

Detective Eric Ashby leaned wearily against the

police cruiser thinking that his boss would screech into the school parking lot, lights and sirens at full bore, inside twenty minutes, which meant he'd better work on getting the security guard composed. The poor man was shaking and trembling and on the verge of collapse and he kept repeating, "I thought it was kids! I thought it was those damn kids again!" And then he'd try to say what he'd seen but the words wouldn't come. "They shot off his... Jesus Christ, somebody shot off his..."

Truth be told, that had been Eric's reaction, too, but duty dictated that he control his horror. After all, what good was a scared cop to a scared public? Especially a cop who'd done such a piss-poor job of working a case that his boss had to leave the office and come out into the field to rescue his sorry ass. Eric allowed himself to wallow fully in his self-pity before dragging himself out of the pit. Anna had explained fully to him — and he trusted and believed her — that they needed to manage carefully a dangerously volatile situation before it blew up in their faces. Three — and now it looked like four — rich and in-the-closet gay people dead and their high-profile unit didn't have the first clue.

He walked back toward the Lincoln, not really needing to see inside again to tell him what was there: Forty-four year old Phillip Tancil, executive vice-president of the Federal Bank of Washington and a resident of Fairfax County, Virginia. The rich part of what was America's richest county. Too bad the license plates of Tancil's car and the DMV computer couldn't ID the killer, too. He stroked the chin that he hadn't had time to shave and thought he should be grateful to Anna for shouldering the burden.

Eric heard the siren and checked his watch: twenty-six minutes. He grinned despite his fatigue as the white unmarked Chevy screeched to a halt on the periphery of the other emergency vehicles, and his grin widened as she stepped from the car as if from the pages of a fashion magazine: chocolate-brown wool slacks and matching sweater topped with a camel hair blazer. She spoke to every cop and ambulance attendant she passed, and lifted a hand in greeting to those out of speaking range. She always did that. Acknowledging the existence of colleagues was a seemingly small thing, but one often ignored by officers of her rank once they'd made it to the top. But she'd always been different. She didn't kowtow to top brass and she didn't shit on the underlings. She treated everybody the same and for that reason everybody liked her. But like is one thing and respect is another and they all respected her because she was a topnotch investigator, some said among the best. She'd earned her Lieutenant's bars and if anybody wondered why a Lieutenant was out working a crime scene in the middle of the night, none of them showed it. She approached Eric and they shared a brief, private look, homage to their long friendship, before she assumed her professional stance.

"You sure it's the same M.O.?" Her low, controlled voice was somehow always soothing, an extension of her presence.

"Exactly like the others, Anna. Guy sitting in his car with his nuts blown all to hell."

7

Eric's tone was bitter, angry, and she knew it was more than mere macho sympathizing. She peered inside the Lincoln, her eyes taking in all the details. Not that she doubted Eric; she had just prayed for him to be wrong. Then she gestured with her eyes toward the security guard seated on the curb with his head in his hands and immediately and correctly summed up who he was: Black man, early fifties, retired government employee who worked the night shift for a private security firm to supplement his pension, probably to put a kid or two through college. She felt sorry for him. He was a guard, not a cop. He wasn't supposed to see things like this.

"He found the victim?"

Eric nodded assent. "Name's Edward Coleman and he's a pure mess. Can't stop shaking."

She nodded at Eric then crossed the several steps to where the guard sat and stooped low to speak to him, placing a hand on his shoulder.

The man raised his head and looked into calm, clear, hazel eyes and stopped his trembling and shaking almost immediately, which was a good thing, because it would be long past dawn before Ed Coleman saw the last of the Hate Crimes Unit of the Metropolitan Police Department.

III

Mimi Patterson squinted at the computer screen. It stared boldly back at her: the same ten sentences comprising the same two paragraphs she'd been looking at for the last twelve minutes. She was having a hard time writing the story on the city council debate on the proposed new junk food tax primarily because she firmly believed that anybody who ate that shit should pay tax on it — not exactly a sterling example of reportorial objectivity. For the one zillionth time in her fifteen-year career she was thankful that the people she covered didn't know what she thought.

"Patterson, you miss deadline and I'll put your butt back on night police!" City Editor Tyler Carson yelled at her across the deadline-tense newsroom.

"Go play in traffic, Tyler," she yelled back, without the slightest enthusiasm or rancor and without removing her eyes from the blue screen with its blinking white cursor. Reporters expected abuse from city editors, and they graciously obliged. And though it was technically within Tyler's power to relegate her to the menial task of prowling around police headquarters on the graveyard shift, it was such an unlikely possibility that Mimi smiled before she could stop herself. She was part of the elite investigative unit and she was riding high after a series of stories detailing scandal at the highest levels of city government that in all likelihood would result in the indictment of a deputy mayor, the head of the city contracting department, and two big construction company honchos. But she well remembered her obligatory three-month stint on night police: she had seen her first murder victim, her first suicide, her first rape victim, her first murderer, her first rapist. And she had learned that unless any of the victims or perps were important people, their stories were not news. They didn't make the paper. But it was necessary to have reporters on that shift because, every now and then, events capable of shaping the course of history occurred in the middle of the night: inept crooks bungle a break-in at the Democratic Party offices and a president is forced to resign; or a congressman's lady-friend goes for a swim in the pond around the corner from the White House, and all of a sudden the whole world's watching. Necessity aside, she would not want to work that shift again; nor would she ever again welcome assignment to the City Desk, to be hassled unmercifully at the same time every day for a story of remarkable sameness to the one of the day before, of the week before, of the month before. And so, as she struggled to make sense of the convoluted candy tax, she silently cursed the filthy flu virus that had felled half the City Desk reporting staff, making her, at this moment, Tyler Carson's victim of choice.

"Patterson, you finished yet?"

"In a minute, Tyler! Keep your shirt on!"

"You've been staring at that screen for a year. What are you looking for, the Holy Grail?"

"Nuance, Tyler. Nuance. But you wouldn't understand."

"Well, you've got ten minutes to find it."

Somebody started singing, "Looking for nuance in all the wrong places," a couple of other people joined in and in the moment, Mimi had what she needed to finish her story.

A little levity makes the world go 'round, she thought, as her fingers tapped a rapid rhythm on the keyboard, the sweetest sound to the ears of the writer. She also thought, briefly, how odd such a situation would seem to someone who required a calm environment in which to formulate thoughts. An unsuspecting being from another planet materializing here would suffer a trauma more serious than culture shock. There was no way to explain a newsroom at deadline to the uninitiated: the sound of three hundred keyboards tapping at breakneck speed; that many phones ringing; that many voices muttering, voices yelling, voices laughing. And the phenomenal accumulation of paper. She remembered the days before computers, the days when news stories were typed on six-ply paper and yet, now that reporters didn't need paper, there seemed to be more of it.

Because of the frantic energy of the newsroom, she knew surely, instinctively, what needed reporting about the junk food tax: it was an issue of economics and health. Kids and poor people were the largest consumers of the sugar-salt-fat-laden category of pre-packaged items called "snack food," and the people least able to afford the higher prices. Yet, the cash-strapped city government desperately needed the extra revenue. So, once again, the budget would be balanced on the backs of the poor.

Mimi looked up at the row of clocks on the wall that told the time for Los Angeles, Chicago, Rome, London, Moscow, Honolulu, Sydney — and Washington — and saw that she had made deadline with several seconds to spare. Then she looked at her desk. At what she could see of it after fourteen weeks of fourteen-hour days spent on the city hall corruption scandal: piles of unopened mail, unanswered telephone messages, unfollowed leads and tips, and the indecipherable-to-anyone-but-her jumble of files that had helped her build the case against yet another crooked politician. It would take the rest of the week to plow through the mess — maybe longer if she got assigned to stay with the junk food tax debate. She permitted herself a brief moment of agitation and irritation, speculating how long it takes to recover from the flu, before she stood, stretched, and gazed across the cavernous newsroom toward Tyler's desk.

She waited, watching while Tyler talked on two phone lines at once, read one story on the computer screen and the wire copy in his hand. He was, she thought, one of the best editors at the paper, one of the best in the business, the kind of authentic editor who'd worked his way up through the reporting ranks. He knew the ins and outs of every story assigned to every reporter who answered to him, and was as good a writer as any of them. Tyler's shortcoming was an absence of personality, which annoyed Mimi. She wanted him to look and act like a dynamic newspaper editor. Instead, he reminded her of her brother-in-law: medium height and medium build with medium brown hair. He wore khaki pants and white shirts and brown knit ties and loafers. Every day. Behind his tortoise shell glasses lived the only sign of life within Tyler: intelligent, intense light green eyes that saw everything. Tyler hung up the phones, eyes riveted to the screen.

"Not a bad story, Patterson, but I wish you wouldn't reduce every issue to the problem of race and class."

"I just call 'em like I see 'em, Tyler. Besides. I said it was a matter of economics and health."

"It means the same thing to you, Patterson. You gotta get over this being Black business."

"Tyler, don't say things like that, even in jest." Mimi spoke calmly and without anger because she had known Tyler long enough and well enough to believe that his comment didn't warrant it. Still, it wasn't the kind of thing to let go without notice.

"Sorry." He hadn't taken his eyes from the computer screen the entire time — no one remembered ever talking to Tyler's eyes.

"So, whaddya think? Will they pass this tax?" he asked the computer screen.

"Yeah. It's not an election year and the city needs the money. Besides, remember who eats that crap, you'll realize it's not the most reliable block of voters." Mimi shrugged and shook her head at the truth of her words.

"You make cynics look like Mary Poppins."

"Yeah. Do I have to do this again tomorrow?"

"Nah. I'll have two of the germ carriers back on duty. Take a casual clothes day tomorrow. Come in late, clean up your desk, get caught up." Tyler waved her away.

Mimi sighed her thanks, looked up at the clocks again, and tried to remember the last time she'd left the paper at seven o'clock in the evening. More than once during the last month, when the corruption investigation was heating up, she had left work at dawn. Several of her best sources would only speak with her, meet with her, deliver the documents crucial to her investigation, in the small hours of the morning.

She switched off the computer and the reading lamp, locked the desk drawer, gathered up her purse and briefcase, still musing that there would actually be people and cars on the street when she left tonight. And it was only Tuesday. There was hope for this week.

Mimi walked out of the building and into the deliciously chilly fall air with a couple of the other reporters, declining their invitation for pizza and beer.

14

After more than a three-month absence, she needed the gym. She'd raised her arm and hailed a taxi before she remembered her car was in the garage. She waved an embarrassed "sorry" to the cabbie who'd swerved across three lanes of traffic to reach her and who shrugged a graceful acceptance of the loss of fare, and walked back into the building, back through the lobby to the rear door and down the back steps, crossing to the farthest corner of the garage where she'd arrogantly angle-parked her red 1969 Karmann Ghia convertible, taking up two spaces.

The car and her 486k turbo computer were the two material possessions about which she cared, that gave her true pleasure. She'd bought her house because her father and her accountant brother-in-law insisted. They'd talked a lot about tax shelters and increasing market value, but she knew they really meant that home ownership was an important safety net for a hard-headed, stubborn, unmarried Black woman of her advanced age. She put the top down, knowing the evening was too chilly but not caring, and backed out of the lot. She popped in a Tina Turner tape and turned up the volume, ready to boogie with the "Private Dancer." She eased the little car into the heavy flow of rush hour traffic, enjoying the current of air that swirled around her and the bombardment of white and red head- and taillights, looking forward to the beauty of nighttime Washington on her crosstown trek.

Washington was a low-to-the-ground city: no skyscrapers here. The law forbade any structure to be taller than the Washington Monument — bane to the real estate developers, boon to those who preferred grass to steel in city living. Washington was a city of wide, tree-lined streets and avenues designed for presidential motorcades: of narrow cobblestoned streets and alleys built for horse-drawn carriages; and engineered in a way that required a stop at practically every intersection. Ancient elms and quietly dignified stone row houses lined block after block, the size of the houses sometimes, though not always, the only indicators of economic status. By the time she reached the quasi-industrial strip of Rhode Island Avenue in the northeast quadrant of the city that housed the gym, she was relaxed and mellow.

An hour into her workout and Mimi felt every one of her thirty-seven years. Her hamstrings quivered and quit in the middle of the third set of leg curls. "I'm too old for this shit," she muttered to herself in perfect imitation of Danny Glover in *Lethal Weapon* as she reduced the weight from forty to thirty-five pounds. Her triceps still burned from the kick backs, and her calves told her not to even try toe raises. Her head agreed with her body, and, stripping en route to the steam room, she pledged a long, leisurely run through Rock Creek Park in the morning since she didn't have to go in to work early.

She threw her clothes into the locker, grabbed a towel from the freshly laundered stack, and was anticipating the relaxing heat of steam when the door opened and out of the mist stepped a woman who caused Mimi's breath to catch in her throat. We are, thought Mimi, looking into clear hazel eyes, exactly the same height. She backed up a step to let the woman pass, and turned to follow with her eyes the perfectly muscled, long-legged body as the woman crossed to the pile of towels. When she turned, she looked directly and coolly into Mimi's eyes; so directly that Mimi was forced to look away. So she looked down, at full perfect breasts, and stopped breathing altogether. Then she turned quickly away, stepped into the steam room and closed the door, thinking that where she really should be was under a cold shower. The heat inside her must have added ten degrees to the temperature in the steam room.

For the remainder of the evening, Mimi puzzled at her reaction to the woman. She'd seen dozens of beautiful — and naked — women. Weight training had been her hobby for the last eight years, and though she had no interest in competition, she thrived on the pure physicality of the sport and enjoyed the camaraderie of the women. And she'd received more than a few admiring — and occasionally lustful — glances at her own physique.

She lay on the couch listening to old Dionne Warwick tapes and seeing again the five feet-eight inches of perfection. Besides, she told herself, she'd never been especially attracted to white women. . . . She closed her eyes and saw the clear, cool hazel gaze and quickly sat upright. "Sex," she said out loud. Dionne said, "Walk on by." Over a year without sex, Mimi reasoned, can make a person behave oddly.

Over a year since her stormy breakup with Beverly. She remembered so clearly Bev's frustration with her unpredictable work schedule; Bev's annoyance that the only activity they routinely shared was Sunday jogging down through Rock Creek Park to the Potomac; and finally, Bev's anger. "All you care about is your precious job and your damn classic car and your souped up computer! And you only want me when it's convenient for you!"

And somewhere deep inside, unwittingly and unwillingly, Mimi had acknowledged the truth of her charge and though she never spoke the words, Bev had heard and all her anger turned, in an instant, to sorrow, and she'd said to Mimi, "Do the women of the world a favor, Mimi, and stay away. Men treat us this way. We don't need it from you. Don't do to another woman what you've done to me."

And Mimi hadn't. She worked her mind and her emotions through her investigative reporting; she worked her body at the gym; and when there was time, she put the top down on the car and took long drives: deep into the lush, gentle Catoctin Mountains of Eastern Maryland or the steeper, more rugged Blue Ridge Mountains of Western Maryland, usually pretending that she was on a country road somewhere in southern Italy....

Mimi squeezed her eyes shut and smacked herself on the forehead in an exaggerated display of recognition of the truth: She was so attracted to the woman because she was Italian! The heavy dark richness of her hair, the hint of olive in her skin, the clear brown of her eyes ... she reminds me of Italy, that's all, thought Mimi with a sigh of relief. Then she saw again the full breasts, the brown of the nipples. She turned face down and pressed herself into the sofa, wondering what in the world she would do about the electric pulsing at the center of her.

IV

Nobody in Homicide, nobody in Forensics, nobody in Pathology or in the ME's office — nobody in the entire bleeping system could ever remember seeing a victim shot in the genitals, and here they had the fourth such victim in as many months — and one of them a woman. They'd bled to death, all four of them, in agonizing, excruciating, paralyzing pain, and then they'd been arranged in their cars — seated upright, hands folded gracefully in their laps.

Lieutenant Maglione sat behind her desk across from the most senior and most junior members of

19

her team. One photograph, of Phillip Tancil seated inside his white Lincoln Town Car, lay face up. She looked at it again, experienced the same sense of revulsion, and returned it to the folder marked "Tancil, P." She had ordered the case files closed to everyone except members of her team and, of course, the department brass, shuddering at the thought of all the gory details being bandied about on the evening news programs. And though the Hate Crimes team understood the rationale for the news blackout, several of them worried about potential fallout.

"Boss, we've got to tell them something," Eric said.

"I don't have to tell them anything," she said matter-of-factly. "The last thing I need in my life is a flock of those vultures hovering around, getting in the way of the investigation." She pushed her chair back from the desk and over close to the window that offered a view of the courthouse flanked by rows of marked and unmarked police vehicles. She briefly looked out, then turned her gaze back to her team, though she did not roll the chair forward.

"Anna, you know what'll happen if they ever get wind of this," Eric said, a look of intense distaste clouding his face.

"Yeah, boss," intoned Cassandra Ali, the youngest member of the team and the resident cynic. "They'll accuse us of covering up information, not cooperating with the press, deceiving the public, and God knows what all."

"I don't give a good damn what the press thinks," the Lieutenant snapped. "We've got a murderer to catch and having those idiots babbling about bullets in the balls won't help us do it."

She heard herself speaking as if she were someone else: the edgy, angry tone so completely out of character that she knew she'd better get herself under control. These crimes had everybody jumpy, even the jaded veterans of homicide and the ME's office who'd seen every kind of crime and victim and who could make a joke out of every cruel circumstance and who usually did, no matter how tasteless or offensive the joke. But nobody was laughing at the brand of depravity that had left four people sitting in their cars in deserted parking lots in the middle of the night with their genitalia blown away by an automatic weapon. Nobody was laughing because these were more than murders; these were like the brand of destruction visited by the crazed gunman who empties his Uzi into a schoolyard full of children or into a crowded restaurant at lunchtime. Nobody was laughing because these were the kinds of crimes that scared cops, even well-seasoned cops like Lieutenant Maglione who, in eighteen years on the force, had worked undercover masquerading as a junkie, a dealer, a hooker, and a for-hire hitman; who had been shot by an illegal alien resisting deportation because he believed jail in America preferable to jail in El Salvador; who had been dumped into the Potomac River in the middle of February by the head of a stolen car ring, an old man angry about being busted by a "fuckin' broad."

Lieutenant Maglione had never, in all those years, through all the danger, been afraid. But she was afraid now, and not because the responsibility for finding the killer fell to her, but because no part of her understood these killings. Murder she understood. Random, senseless violence she understood. Even cold, calculated, motivated crime she understood. But the deliberate humiliation by mutilation in the most personal and intimate of ways — this was something different. There was no way she could remain locked inside her office, directing the investigation by reading reports.

She rolled the chair back to the desk and opened the Tancil file, the image of death still right there on top.

"Do we know for sure this latest guy was gay?"

"Not yet, Anna, but can there be any doubt —"

"That's just the point, Eric. There can be no doubt. Either we're looking for somebody who systematically, deliberately and specifically kills gay people in cars in parking lots at midnight, on the same day of the month, or we're not."

"But you can't really think we've got a copycat killer?" Cassandra looked at her in youthful, wide-eyed amazement.

"We can't afford to think anything, Cassie, we've got to be certain." But the possibility of a copycat killer was another major reason for a press blackout. With all the hate in this city, details of this newest horror could tip borderline psychos over the edge. Better to present the press with the arrest of the killer, and the public with the knowledge that monsters would be hunted down and apprehended. She continued, "Suppose our killer thought Phil Tancil was gay and he wasn't? Suppose Liz Grayson was an accident . . ."

"Dammit, Anna!" Eric jumped to his feet and

stalked about the cramped office. "Elizabeth Grayson was a lesbian and she was shot in the ba — in the genitals like the guys! How can you think she was an accident? She's part of the pattern!"

"Eric, we're playing catch up here. We're the scrub team, thrown into the game in the third period to clean up the mess the big guys made. If we win, we got lucky. If we don't, we're the assholes the big guys always thought we were. Either way we're walking uphill in cement boots." She was still smarting over the fact that the Hate Crimes Unit hadn't been assigned to the case until after the third murder, when Homicide realized that all the victims were gay. By that time, information, interviews and people's memories were three months old.

"Your confidence is inspiring, oh great leader."

Eric deserved his right to sarcasm and she grinned her acceptance at him.

"We've pulled out all the stops on this thing, Anna. We know everything there is to know about these victims —"

She interrupted him gently but firmly. "No, Eric, we don't. We don't know why these four people are dead."

"Dammit, Anna, they're dead because they're gay!"

"That's a factor, but it's not the reason." She stood so abruptly that the chair rolled backward, crashing solidly into the radiator beneath the window. "The truth is, not only don't we know the reason for these murders, we're nowhere close to finding out." She was very still, her voice low and controlled, and it had the desired effect of calming and quieting him. He squeezed his eyes shut and rubbed his forehead. Cassandra, barely breathing, looked from one to the other of her superiors, waiting.

"Homicide treated these cases as ordinary murders, meaning they only looked for clues that would lead them to a killer —"

"Don't we have to do the same thing?" Cassandra ventured.

"No, Cassie, we don't and we can't. These specific people were killed in a specific way for a specific reason. We have to find that reason. If it's as simple a matter as sexual preference, why doesn't the killer drive by Traks or DuPont Circle or P Street Beach or Badlands on any given Friday or Saturday and just open fire?"

Calmer now, Eric continued with his report. "We've had people on Tancil's background around the clock. His wife seems not to understand the word 'homosexual' any more than the people at his job. Totally foreign concept. But there's this group he golfed with every weekend and if there's a crack in the wall, that's where it'll be." Eric added wearily, "We should have some word pretty soon."

Cassie, her boss noted, had observed this rare public conflict between superiors in guarded silence. Now she exhaled deeply, apparently relieved at the break in the tension. Exhibiting a degree of intuition rare in one so young but crucial to expert police work, she stood up and made for the door.

"The pseudo-intellectuals at the lab called me a nuisance and threw me out, but screw 'em. I think I'll go harass 'em some more. See you guys later." She closed the door silently behind her.

Anna retrieved her errant chair, leaned back

gratefully, and put her feet on the desk. "So. Eric. What's really bugging you?"

"You know me too well," he said with a rueful smile.

She returned the smile. They'd known each other for almost twenty years — they'd been in the same Training Academy class and had become fast friends one night during a celebration party after a big exam. Eric had come swiftly and forcefully to her rescue when one of their classmates drunkenly accused her of being the dyke she was when she resisted his advances. Later, Eric explained that a childhood of defending an effeminate older brother against schoolyard toughs had made him totally intolerant of those who attacked people because they were, simply, who and what they were. They'd maintained and nourished their friendship even though they worked different details and different shifts, and when she was selected to head up the newly created Hate Crimes Unit, she'd chosen him to be her second in command, not only because he was her friend, or even because he was a good cop, but because his anger complemented hers and between the two of them they got things done: the hotter his anger burned the icier she became. With his unruly bright red hair and his brilliant bright blue eyes, he looked like a choirboy but was one of the toughest, hardest cops she'd ever seen, and his overflowing fury at the brutality of these crimes matched her own seething anger.

"These people thought they were safe, Anna. They thought their lives were their own. They were wrong and now they're dead and that scares the hell out of me and I know it scares you just as much."

"I've been trying not to think about that aspect of it. I can't catch a killer if I'm spending time worried about keeping my own closet door locked."

She had struggled mightily to keep those thoughts from her consciousness. What she allowed herself to think was that the killer had used the same .45 calibre gun for all four murders — and a damn big gun it was, too, to obliterate so thoroughly and savagely. She allowed herself to wonder why Phillip Tancil — why any of the victims — would let somebody with so powerful a gun into the front seat of their cars with them, for there was no evidence of forced entry into any of the victims' vehicles. And she allowed herself, finally, to wonder how many more people would die before she found the answers to those questions. But she didn't say any of those things to Eric.

"Why is it that only on TV are murderers dumb?" she asked rhetorically. "If real life followed the TV scripts, by now we should have all kinds of clues and our killer should be suffering from a guilty conscience and ready to surrender." She smiled but it was bleak and didn't really lift either of them.

Eric said, "But we do get a little more each time, Anna. We do get just a little closer . . ."

She thought about how very far she was from understanding these murders and a shudder of dread ran through her. As much as she wanted to quiet Eric's fears, her own would not permit it.

"It's not enough, pal. Not nearly enough."

By the time Mimi finished filling the second bag

of trash, she could see the top of her desk. She could also see how much of life she'd missed while engrossed in this latest investigation: a half dozen invitations to cocktail parties; a request to sponsor a friend in the AIDS Walk; a personal invitation from the Chief of Police to meet the female Lieutenant heading the newly created Hate Crimes Section; a plea from her sorority to attend its annual scholarship dinner; a request to lend her name to a United Negro College Fund solicitation; a 10K charity run to benefit the shelter for battered women. She made a note to send checks to the UNCF, the shelter, the sorority, and the AIDS hospice, tossed the invitations in the trash, and stood up to haul the bag across the newsroom to the recycling bin. From behind her came a low, slow wolf whistle. She'd stopped paying any attention to Len Broward about ten years ago, so she didn't even turn around.

"How long did it take to pour yourself into those Levis, Patterson?" Len whistled again as she dragged the bag of trash away.

Mimi knew the jeans were tight but after last night's humbling experience at the gym, she needed to prove to herself that they still fit, that her body was still the well-honed, perfectly sculpted specimen she'd spent the last eight years creating. She'd have preferred notice from somebody other than Len.

"Patterson! See you a minute?"

She ambled to Tyler's desk, wondering whether her day to get caught up was over so soon.

"You free for lunch?"

"Lunch?" She was genuinely surprised by the question.

"Lunch, Patterson. Food. Something most of us eat. Though judging by the size of those Levis, I'd say it's not something you do on a regular basis."

Mimi grinned. "Yeah, Tyler, I'm available, though I wish you'd asked me on a day when I was more appropriately dressed."

"Since when do you worry about protocol?"

She shrugged in admission of his correct perception.

"Besides, you look better than most of the people who're supposed to be dressed for work. Meet you in the lobby at one-thirty."

"I'll be there," she said, sauntering back to her desk. She was struck by the fact that Tyler had actually looked at her while he talked, looked her in the eyes, noticed her clothes. Something is up, she thought, something big. Tyler wouldn't take her to lunch on the expense account at the hoity-toity Le Petit Paris favored by the newspaper execs if something major weren't in the air. She looked down at herself — the honey-colored silk blouse, the clean if very tight Levis, the blue suede loafers, the fawn-colored soft suede jacket hanging on the back of her chair — and remembered that her first impulse had been to wear sneakers and a sweatshirt to work.

Mimi and Tyler walked out into the crisp air and she slammed into him when she turned right, en route to Le Petit Paris.

"Walk much, Patterson?" growled Tyler. She was

forming her retort when he raised his arm to hail a taxi.

"We're not going to the Frenchery?"

"Obviously," he drawled as a Red and Black taxi cut off a Yellow cab and screeched to halt, the driver of the Yellow cab cursing mightily in Spanish. Tyler gave the driver the address of a quaint, quiet Italian restaurant on Dupont Circle known to specialize in the cooking of Southern Italy. It was also known to have a substantial gay clientele . . .

Her thoughts were a jumble when Tyler broke the silence. "You see the story this morning about the banker found in the Washington High parking lot?"

She vaguely recalled the item, buried deep inside the Region section: white male, forties, bank president, shot to death in his car in a parking lot more than twenty miles from his Fairfax County home. No motive, no suspects, no big deal, she thought. After all, the Nation's capital was the murder capital of America. But before she could say any of this, Tyler asked if she'd read about three other murders of successful business people, all in their forties, all well-connected politically and socially. Mimi didn't remember, didn't know why she should, and said as much to Tyler. He grunted and agreed that on the surface, there seemed to be nothing outstanding about any of the crimes. Then he stopped talking and Mimi knew he would say nothing more in the taxi. She knew his questions were relevant, but she didn't see how four apparently unconnected murders . . . unless they were connected . . .

* * * * *

"Patterson, are you gay?" Mimi choked on a big gulp of San Pellegrino and glared at Tyler.

"I have an important reason for asking," he said carefully.

"You damn well better," she coughed, still choking a bit.

"I need you to answer first, Mimi."

He had never, ever called her Mimi. She studied him, thinking about the position she'd taken regarding her sexuality years ago: *I'll never respond to innuendo or rumor, but if anyone is ever honest enough to ask me a direct question, I'll give 'em a direct answer.*

"Yes, Tyler, I am. Now, explain this invasion of my privacy."

"The four murders I mentioned. One each month, on the same day of the month, the last four months. They were all gay. All of them were married, had children, important jobs — powerful jobs — and all of them were gay. Deeply closeted."

Tyler played with his food, waiting for her response. She tried to remember something, anything about the murders, but they'd occurred while she was engrossed in her investigation — except for the latest one on Monday night. She tried to make her mind imagine all the implications of what she'd just heard, and her mind rebelled at the horror of it. *There's a monster out there.*

"So, I guess you know what your next assignment is."

"I'll start this afternoon."

"No. I want you spend the rest of this week

30

catching up. Clear your desk, answer your mail, return your phone calls, get plugged back in, find your balance. Start this on Monday."

She started to protest, then remembered something. "Do the police know these people were gay?"

"I don't think so. Why?" Tyler frowned at her.

"Then how do you know?"

"Monday night's victim was a friend. The first one, four months ago, was the friend of a friend. On a hunch, I asked a pal at the FBI to look at the other two..."

He trailed off and Mimi looked at him closely, intensely. He raised his eyes to meet hers. "Yes, I'm gay, too. Feel better?" Tyler smiled slightly.

"I feel like shit, thank you," Mimi growled at him. "Now I get to worry that next month this time the victim may be one of my friends." She looked down at the plate of penne primavera for which she now had no appetite and was able to take solace only in the fact that somebody else would have to pay for the wasted meal.

Mimi tried to concentrate on clearing up old business, as Tyler said, but the new assignment tugged at her until she eventually gave in and grabbed the phone.

"This is Montgomery Patterson. I'd like to make an appointment to see Lieutenant Maglione." Mimi sighed heavily into the dead space that meant she was on hold, as much a Washington institution as the Lincoln or the Jefferson monuments. She disliked

31

calling the police department. Some of D.C.'s finest still resented her for exposing a cell of rogue cops guilty of everything from police brutality to drug dealing. They had called themselves The Avengers and saw it as their mission to rid the city of drug dealers, murderers, and other negative elements; and in their zeal, they became exactly as warped and twisted as those they professed to hate. Most police department personnel, including the Chief, were relieved to be rid of the bad apples; but some cops still adhered to a code that protected a fellow officer no matter what, and it rankled her whenever she encountered hostility from the Public Affairs officer, and she almost regretted making the call. But in a few moments he was back on the line with the information that she could meet the new Hate Crimes boss in her office at eleven o'clock Monday morning.

For the remainder of that week, Mimi left work every day at seven and went directly to the gym where she had a sweat-popping workout followed by leisurely steam. But no matter how much she willed it, The Woman did not reappear. Saturday she cleaned her house, ridding it of all traces of the previous investigation. She downloaded all the old files from her computer and opened a new one with a new password for the murder cases. And on the wall above her desk she hung the pictures of the four murder victims that Tyler had somehow gotten from his FBI pal: a white man, a Black man, an Hispanic man, and a white woman, their success and their sexuality their only links to each other. Could it really be true, she wondered, studying the faces, that these people were dead because of who they loved? And somehow she knew the answer was yes.

Mimi awoke early Sunday, read the paper from cover to cover, then rode her bicycle through Rock Creek Park to the Kennedy Center where she parked and locked it and began her run toward and across the Potomac River via the Memorial Bridge. It was a brilliant day, the towering oak and elm and maple trees resplendent in their fall reds and golds. It was still early enough that there were no crowds and Mimi ran easily, at a moderate pace, marveling as always at the magnificence of the trees and the shimmering reflection of the sun on the placid surface of the water. Then she saw two women walking toward her, their jerseys wet with sweat. They'd finished their run, must've been out early.... Great Christ Almighty! Beverly, with her lovely long dreadlocks gathered in a bright scarf, and The Woman from the gym!

Mimi slowed as she approached them, then stopped, reached out for Bev and brushed her lips with a gentle kiss. "Hi, Bev. You're out early. Don't tell me you've changed."

"Not a chance and not my idea. Gianna likes running this early." Bev looked quizzically at Mimi and asked, "You two know each other?"

"Ah, not exactly ..." Mimi began, as Bev made the introduction utilizing the correct Italian pronunciation of the name: Giovanna Maglione, Gianna to her friends. She *is* Italian, thought Mimi, looking into the hazel eyes, exchanging a firm handshake. And she is beautiful.

"Good to meet you, Mimi," Gianna said, a hint of a smile at the corners of her mouth.

"Too bad you're just getting started. I'd ask you to join us for brunch," Bev said.

"Maybe we can all take a raincheck on brunch," Mimi said, leaning toward Bev to kiss her again. "You look good, Bev," she said. And directly to the hazel eyes she said, "Ciao, Bella."

Mimi jogged off, aware that two pairs of eyes followed her.

"Beverly! That's the Mimi you left? That's the one?"

"That's the one," Bev said with a small smile.

"She's gorgeous!" said Gianna, still watching Mimi run.

"She is that. And brilliant and witty and charming and . . ."

". . . And you're still in love with her," Gianna prodded.

"No, I'm not. I've got some places that haven't healed from her yet, but I'm not still in love with her."

Gianna was surprised by her relief at those words. She and Beverly were new friends, not yet close, but they liked each other, and Gianna, who wanted and needed a good friend, thought they could be close with time. But not with an ex-lover like Mimi standing between them. Why, she wondered, had Bev left? Other women? Gianna remembered opening the steam room door and almost colliding with Mimi. Their bodies were so close . . . Gianna still

34

felt the heat. Other women would certainly be attracted.

"Why did you leave her, Bev?"

"I don't want to talk about Mimi, Lieutenant. Okay?"

"Oh, low blow. But I get the message."

She looked at the reporter sitting on the other side of her desk and wished she had pressed Bev further. That way she wouldn't have felt so total a fool at the sight of investigative reporter M. Montgomery Patterson, aka Mimi.

They'd stood looking at each other, waiting for the secretary to leave and close the door. Then they laughed.

Gianna seized control of her turf. "Miss Patterson. Mimi. Please sit down. It really is a pleasure to meet you. You do good work."

"Thank you, Lieutenant. Congratulations on your promotion and sorry I missed the party."

"So was the Chief. He kept telling me how much I'd like you." She smiled a half smile that made Mimi feel somebody had turned up the heat in the office.

"I wish the Chief would work on his Italian. He butchered your name. I had no idea what I was walking into."

"Not even when Bev introduced us? No little bell rang?"

"I confess that the sight of the two of you together yesterday erased every other thought from my head," Mimi said fervently. Gianna laughed again and Mimi struggled to keep her mind on work.

"So, is this a duty call, to satisfy the Chief?"

Mimi hesitated, wondering if she should back into the reason for her visit or jump in with both feet. Gianna looked like a jump in kind of woman.

"I'm investigating the murders of Elizabeth Grayson, Joseph Murray, Phillip Tancil and Antonio delValle."

An absolute stillness settled over Gianna. She didn't move a muscle, didn't blink an eye, didn't take an extra breath. She even managed a small and condescending smile when she said in her controlled voice, "But this isn't Homicide, Miss Patterson."

"I know exactly what this is, Lieutenant. Are you telling me the Hate Crimes Unit isn't investigating the murders of those four people?"

"I'm telling you that Homicide investigates murder," Gianna said carefully, and held Mimi's stare.

Mimi broke eye contact first and took a slow, deliberate look around the small, neat office, her eyes resting longest on the photograph of a young man in a policeman's uniform from another city and another era.

A rap on the door broke the tension. Before Gianna could even think "come in," the door burst open and the Chief of Police was propelled in by the force of his own energy. He was not a tall man — he stood an inch under six feet — but he had the tight, compact body of the Golden Gloves boxer he'd been in his youth and he walked on the balls of his feet so that he seemed taller and he always conveyed the impression of moving forward. He was made to wear the midnight-blue and gold of a police chief and he wore it well. Both women stood and Gianna showed genuine surprise when the Chief wrapped Mimi in a bear hug and kissed her on both cheeks.

"You need a haircut, Mimi. Otherwise you're just as beautiful as ever. You two enjoying each other?" He barked at them in the rapid-fire staccato that had made people heed his words his entire career.

"Absolutely," Mimi said, "and I'm glad to see you finally did something right, making Lieutenant Maglione head of Hate Crimes."

"Funny. That's what she said. I knew you two would get along. You're a lot alike. Well, I've gotta go make a speech. I envy you two, you still get to chase the bad guys while I get to eat rubber chicken and try to explain why we can't catch every drug dealer, murderer and rapist before they commit their crimes. And by the way, Lieutenant, I hear you're not acting very much like a Lieutenant. That's not good for my image, you know." And he left as abruptly as he had arrived.

Mimi and Gianna shared a look of amazement. "What did he mean by that crack?" Mimi asked, eyebrows raised.

Gianna waved away the question with one of her own. "How do you know him like that?" she asked, laughing.

"When I was new to the paper, new in town, all of twenty-two years old and stuck on night police, he took care of me. He was Homicide then, and stumbled upon me literally moments after I'd seen my first murder victim."

Gianna watched her remember, watched her eyes

recede to the past, watched her face soften and become that of a scared cub reporter. She listened to the voice lose its hard reporter's edge as it recalled that other, simpler time, when a young woman became an adult virtually overnight. And she was irritated when the phone buzzed, snatching them both back to the here and now. She grabbed it up, listened, spoke a few words Mimi couldn't hear even though she was just a few feet away, and hung up.

"Well, back to the grind for me," Gianna said briskly. She walked around her desk.

Mimi thought again, we are exactly the same height. She appraised Gianna in her uniform, the military precision of the garb, so perfect for the Chief, not coming close to complementing Gianna — the dark blue jacket and skirt and the crisp white shirt too stiff and unyielding for the form beneath ... The rich, dark hair unsuccessfully tamed by pins and barrettes ...

Gianna extended her hand and Mimi kept it a fraction of a second longer than necessary before turning to exit. She had one foot in the hall when she heard her name.

Gianna, smiling, said softly, "I like your hair like that," and then she closed the door and Mimi, too charged to wait for the elevator, raced down the stairs, taking them two at a time, her mind in overdrive as she was jostled about in the teeming lobby of police headquarters.

Mimi was deciding to take the subway instead of a taxi so she'd have more time to think: Gianna Maglione sure as hell knew those four people were gay. What else did she know? Was there something about the murders the cops were keeping secret, some little piece of information only the killer would know?

And what was that business about her hair? If it was designed to distract her . . . well, it had worked. Mimi made a mental note to cancel next Tuesday's appointment with the guy who cut her hair.

Gianna crossed to the window and looked down on the block that comprised Judiciary Square — an enclave that held the local courts, the city jail and police headquarters at one end, and the Federal courthouses at the other. Cops and lawyers and the people who kept them in business resembled a colony of ants streaming in and out of the various buildings, looking as if they were engaged in some industrious pursuit rather than in games of crime. The gleaming white marble-and-chrome of the newer buildings stood in stark contrast to the unpolished brass and crumbling brick of the older ones, a testament to the changes wrought in the thing called the law. As she watched the scene below, Gianna played an old game with herself: who were the undercover cops and who were the perps? It got harder and harder to tell.

Mimi appeared on the sidewalk, merged with the crowd, and joined the ant column inching toward the subway, and Gianna wondered what had compelled her to make the comment about Mimi's hair, and as she wondered, Gianna could see her, feel her, smell her, as if she were still standing in the office, much too close for comfort. Then she remembered the first time she saw her, naked in the steam; she remembered the strength and power of her legs as she jogged and the tenderness with which she kissed Beverly. And she remembered that she was due at a meeting with the M.E. and she closed her eyes tightly, hoping to still the sharp, aching desire pulsing at her center.

V

"Let me tell you people that you've got one big mess on your hands. As much as we'd all like to believe it, these crimes are not about sex, pure and simple." Dr. Asa Shehee was the city's — and the nation's — leading forensic psychiatrist.

"Pure? Simple?" Gianna snorted in disgust. She'd asked Shehee to come here because she wanted the newer members of her team to encounter the irascible old legend on neutral turf. He'd obliged because he'd known her for over a decade, and

41

because he believed that young cops had nowhere near enough understanding and respect for the science of forensics.

"Don't shoot the messenger," Shehee growled, lumbering about like the grizzly that he resembled.

Gianna marveled that he'd somehow found room to pace in the cramped space that the Hate Crimes team referred to as the Think Tank — really a small conference room on the floor directly below Gianna's office, equipped with a long, beat-up table, a dozen dented folding chairs, and a pair of wooden four-drawer file cabinets that Gianna swore had existed before the Police Department did. A blackboard ran the length of one wall and a screen was mounted on the adjacent wall on which the Team projected crime scene images. The only relatively modern, relatively new tools housed in the Think Tank were a television and VCR, and a computer that crashed with painful regularity.

The Hate Crimes team watched Shehee intently, the faces of the younger ones eager and fascinated; the faces of the veterans tight with dread.

"Obliterating the genitalia makes one hell of a statement. And you can count on some kind of religious motivation," he added, running stubby, tobacco-stained fingers through spiky white hair, still pacing and electrically charging the air in the close room.

"Because of the way the hands were folded?" Gianna asked.

"Yep. And I'll tell you something else. You people better hunker down for the long haul. This is a real sicko, but a really smart sicko and he won't make many mistakes."

Gianna grimaced. "He's already made one," she said, steely voiced.

"What's that?" Shehee demanded.

"He's let us know he hates homosexuals."

Shehee's grunt sounded exactly like that of an angry bear. "This bastard hates life and the living," he rumbled.

After the forensics man left, Gianna took up his pacing. She couldn't stop wondering what kind of mind could perpetrate so horrible, so painful, so torturous a death, and then, after watching the victims expire, fold their hands over the bloody mess. *He hates homosexuals,* she thought. *He hates life and the living.* Shehee's growly voice reverberated inside her brain. *A real sicko.*

She spent the weekend poring over psychiatric profiles of serial killers, hoping to find a hint of an answer.

Mimi spent the weekend a hundred and fifty miles from Washington, in Western Maryland, in a cabin on Deep Creek Lake owned by her best friend, Freddy Schuyler, a former Washington Redskins offensive tackle and current owner of the hottest nightclub in D.C. They'd been friends since college, when, after a few dates, they realized each other's truth. They liked each other as friends and didn't want to pursue the mating charade. They became inseparable, allowing people to think what they wished while they blissfully double-dated with their respective lovers. That they'd both ended up in Washington had been purely miraculous.

They now sat on the floor before the stone fireplace that spanned an entire wall of the cabin, drinking champagne and eating popcorn. Mimi filled Freddy in on the story — she always told him everything about every investigation so that in case something went wrong, somebody would know what she was working on. She also respected his views and his values.

"Why those four people?" she demanded. "It's not like they were leading ACT UP demonstrations. They were deep in the closet."

"You know better than to look for logic in these situations. Look at that deputy mayor you just busted. Why in the hell would he think he could run that kind of scam and get away with it? Why does anybody care who anybody else loves?"

They watched the flames flicker and leap and dance. Then he said, "Anyway, I'm more worried right now about people who're supposed to be on my side than about unseen enemies. Talk about crazies!" Freddy slapped his thigh in irritation. "These outing people are about to drive me insane!"

"The what people?"

"Outing. Where the hell have you been, Mimi? There is other news than the stories you write, you know. Outing, as in out of the closet . . ."

"You mean that group trying to make the gay movie stars 'fess up? That's Hollywood, Freddy."

"Tell that to the two creeps who keep bugging me about coming out. Young athletes need me as a role model, they say. They've threatened to yank open my closet door if I don't voluntarily —"

"But that's . . . they can't do that! That could destroy your business!" Mimi was appalled.

"You're telling me?" A glum Freddy got up to open another bottle of champagne and when he returned to the hearth, his equilibrium was restored.

"Drink a toast to me, darling Mimi. While you were rounding up the bad guys, I was falling in love. His name's Cedric, he's British, he teaches poetry at Rutgers, and I want you to meet him. Can you imagine a Black guy named Cee-drick? And a poet? Good thing he didn't grow up in my South Central Los Angeles neighborhood."

Mimi laughed at Freddy's excitement and hugged him close, privately cursing the myopic narrow-mindedness that had prevented so many men from seeing the warm, gentle spirit who lived inside Freddy Schuyler's football-player body. She held him as he told her how, after a three month courtship, they'd gone together for an AIDS test, promising to stay together no matter what the results.

"I have no words to describe the feeling when we both got our negative results. It was like being born again, Mimi."

"I'm so happy for you," she said, brushing away tears. "And I can't wait to meet him."

"Next Saturday night. I'll cook. Vegetarian lasagna, just for you."

Surprised, she said, "You're taking two weekends in a row off from the nightclub?"

He shrugged, the gloom settling back over him. "I'm supposed to be outed next weekend. I thought maybe if I wasn't there. . . ."

"Dammit, Anna, stop being so bullheaded!"

"Trying to catch a murderer, trying to save you and me and the department major embarrassment, trying to keep our collective butts out of a sling — that's being bullheaded? Oh, well, excuuuuuse me."

Her sarcasm was as half-hearted as her boss's ire. They faced each other across his massive oak desk stacked high with piles of papers and reports and crime stats. Captain Eddie Davis was head of Criminal Intelligence, to which the Hate Crimes Unit and Gianna reported, and she knew he had no earthly idea that she was thinking, as she looked at him, not about the four unsolved murders plaguing them, but how very much he resembled Sidney Poitier. She suspected it was the foremost thought in the mind of every woman he encountered, and he'd heard it so often that he no longer paid attention when people said it to him.

"I understand your rationale, Anna, believe me I do. But it causes ripples for you to be getting your hands dirty out in the field on this case. You need to be a presence inside the Shop. The big boys need to see you in here looking like you're in charge, not bleary-eyed and exhausted from being out until four in the morning like one of your officers."

Davis even spoke in calm, measured tones, just like Poitier, she thought, studying him.

"Am I boring you, Lieutenant?" Davis' eyebrows edged up.

"No, sir. I was thinking about what you said. I can't argue. I can only tell you I don't believe we can work this case like these are regular, run-of-the-mill murders." She followed his eyes as they traveled to her report and she knew he'd read every word, that he was as familiar with the case as

46

she. She also knew he did a good job of reading between the lines and understood that she'd been greatly hampered by not receiving the case until after the third murder — which was when Homicide realized that what they had was more than just murder — and that Hate Crimes had been playing catch-up ever since.

"I agree, Anna, that your back is against the wall. This is the damnedest thing I believe I've ever seen. Still . . . do me a favor, will you? Just act like you're being a desk jockey and loving it, okay?" He grinned when he said it but she knew he meant it.

"Okay," she said, returning his grin. "If you'll do one for me." His eyes narrowed slightly but he nodded. "Back me up on the media blackout."

"Hell yes!" he exploded. "I'm with you all the way on that one. We don't need the press on this case."

Mimi thumbed through the stacks of files about outing piled on her desk, alternating between anger and dismay. How could one gay person not understand, not respect, the unwillingness or the inability of another to come out? Being queer in America, she thought wryly, was one of the few things worse than being Black. It was possible to be forgiven the color of one's skin, the assumption being that one had no choice in the matter. But to love one's same sex — that was something else. No matter how hotly the debate raged in medical and scientific circles, a significant proportion of the population seemed to think that gay people needed only to decide to stop being gay and that was that. Mimi didn't know of a single person who had delighted in informing his or her family/friends/colleagues/clients/patients/landlord/employer of the fact of his or her gayness. She sighed and tossed the files aside. In terms of the investigation she'd been assigned, outers outraged people but they didn't kill them.

She paged through the files she'd compiled on the four murder victims. The twenty-first day of July, August, September and October — Murray, delValle, Grayson and Tancil, killed in that order. They'd all married in their twenties, either before understanding fully the truth of their sexuality, or believing a conventional marriage the only option. They had all lived in the wealthiest sections of the Maryland and Virginia suburbs that surrounded Washington, but each was murdered far from home, in a darkened parking lot or garage inside the city.

She tossed the files aside in irritation. What she had was virtually nothing and what she needed was hard information. She reached for the phone, hesitated, then resolutely dialed.

"Lieutenant Maglione, please. This is Montgomery Patterson." Her heart rate increased when the composed voice answered.

"Miss Patterson. How can I help?"

She's so remote, Mimi thought. Maybe somebody's with her. "Can you tell me, please Lieutenant, how Mrs. Grayson, Mr. Tancil, Mr. Murray and Mr. delValle all happened to be in those parking lots so late at night?"

There was the slightest pause before Gianna responded. "I'm afraid you have me at a disadvantage, Miss Patterson, since only you know what you're talking about."

48

Mimi smiled in spite of herself. "You're good, Lieutenant. Very good. Will you at least tell me how much longer you think we'll have to play games with each other about this case?"

"I take it you mean the case I haven't acknowledged exists?"

"You can acknowledge its existence or I can file an FOI for access to the case information," Mimi snapped. "Tell me what you'd like me to do, Lieutenant."

"I'd like for you to have a very pleasant day, Miss Patterson."

Gianna winced and jerked the phone away from her ear as Mimi slammed it down on the other end. She smiled wanly at Eric, who was seated across the desk, feet up, eating a turkey sandwich and reading the lab report on the Tancil car. Gianna rotated her neck, hoping to ease the knot of tension that had taken up permanent residence.

"A reporter somehow knows about Grayson, Tancil, et al."

Eric got sandwich caught in his throat and coughed before he could speak. "Knows? Knows what? Knows they were all gay? How is that possible? It's not possible!"

"I don't know how she knows, but Montgomery Patterson is privy to that information. I can only be thankful that if a reporter must know, it's her. At least she won't rush to print without all the facts."

"Are you sure?"

"The only thing I'm sure about, Eric, is that I don't know where this came from or where it's going."

"But that's not exactly true, is it?" His brow

creased in earnestness. "I mean, we know with some certainty that —"

She interrupted him impatiently. "You and Cassie finish going over the psychiatric profiles and keep bugging Homicide about the interview reports they claim they can't find." Almost as an afterthought she added, "And have a set of purged files delivered to Montgomery Patterson."

"You really want to give her files?" he asked incredulously.

"I'm just giving her what she already knows, and I'd rather do that than have her arousing interest by filing a Freedom of Information Act request. Every reporter in town would jump on that bandwagon."

Eric tossed her a half salute and ambled out. She sat quietly, thinking about Mimi Patterson. Sooner or later they'd have to talk about the case. More precisely, Gianna would have to divulge facts in order to find out what the reporter knew and from what source. She'd never had much dealing with the press and she had been warned that her promotion would change all that. At least half the job of heading up a major crimes unit, the Chief had told her, was public relations.

But she hadn't figured on M. Montgomery Patterson. . . . She pushed the image of Mimi out of her mind, Mimi naked, her smooth, burnished umber skin so close to her, the heat between them not all from the steam room. She closed her eyes to Mimi and opened them to the files before her to the horrible, depraved ugliness that would consume her until she found and stopped him-her-those responsible.

What in these files would lead her to the killer?

What, if anything, did she — the officer in charge of the investigation — know that Mimi Patterson, the reporter, did not know? Not a hell of a lot. That Phil Tancil's wife had become hysterical when confronted with her husband's homosexuality, and so angry that Gianna had feared being assaulted by her. She'd refused to discuss it, refused to permit a search of his personal belongings, accused the police of tarnishing the image of a good family man, and called her lawyer when Gianna obtained a search warrant. She could not and would not understand why the police needed to know the tiniest details of a victim's background in order to find his killer and she refused to join any speculation about the reasons for his presence in the Washington High School parking lot well after midnight on a Monday night.

Joe Murray's wife had responded in exactly the opposite manner. Eerily calm, she told Gianna she'd known Joe was hiding something, that he was carrying some weight that often made him aloof and distant for long periods of time. Her worst fear, she told Gianna, was that Joe was engaged in some illegal activity, because she hadn't fully understood that her husband's consulting firm was as successful as he claimed it was, and she'd wondered where all the money came from. She allowed Gianna and her team full access to Joe's home and office safes where he kept his private papers but insisted that the Murray children know nothing of their father's homosexuality. Why would Joe Murray be in the deserted, cavernous parking lot of RFK Stadium at midnight? "He loved the Redskins," she said with a resigned shrug. And did she believe, Gianna had asked gently, that Joe's murder could be sexually oriented? "It would appear so," she'd answered with painful honesty.

Tony delValle's wife was angry. She'd known of her husband's homosexuality for years. They'd seen therapists and counselors together and separately and Tony would give up men for a while but only for a while, until the AIDS scare, and she had believed Tony's promise that he was "out of the life for good." He'd said he was afraid of AIDS, and he knew that his habit of meeting men in bars and movie houses endangered himself and his family. "And now I find out in the worst way that he lied to me." She spat out the words.

Gianna probed, "So you think your husband's murder was tied to his sexual activities?"

The woman's pain and anger boiled over. "He was driving a forty-thousand-dollar car. He was wearing five thousand dollars worth of jewelry. He had almost five hundred dollars in his pocket. Do you think I'm stupid, lady? Whoever killed him didn't do it for money!" Gianna accepted the full force of the woman's fury because she could do no less.

It was Liz Grayson's husband who gave Gianna the first bit of information that resembled a lead. Harry Grayson, a tall, thin handsome man in his late forties, longish hair almost totally silver, had known for years of his wife's attraction to and involvement with women, but he also knew that she was much too conventional to try and face the world without her husband and children. They were her protection, her insulation, and she would do nothing to jeopardize that. She was not promiscuous, he insisted, but rather became engaged in long term affairs — most recently with Susan Jolley, a computer analyst for the Army. They'd stopped seeing each other about a month before Liz was killed, he said, because of threats made by Susan's ex-lover, a woman named Karen.

"What kind of threats, Mr. Grayson?" She touched his arm as tears filled his eyes, spilled down his cheeks.

He removed the silver-edged half glasses but allowed the tears to flow unchecked. The navy corduroy slacks and turtleneck sweater he wore perfectly complemented the image of the research scientist that he was. "The kind I now know to take seriously. This Karen threatened to kill Liz because she thought Liz took Susan away from her."

Harry Grayson looked helplessly around the homey den filled with soft, rich furniture and photographs of himself and his wife and their children and other family members. "I can't believe she's gone, Lieutenant." And he wiped tears with the back of his hand.

Susan Jolley was also gone, had disappeared. Quit her job, sold her car, emptied her bank account, vanished. These little bits of information the police investigator did not share with the investigative reporter; instead she stingily kept them close, guarding them, in case one of the bits ripened and bore fruit — the hard, bitter fruit that leads, eventually and ultimately, to a murderer.

"You've only been on the story a week and a half, Patterson. What makes you think you should have all the answers already? Starting to believe your own press?" His lively green eyes studied her across the narrow booth in the loud, crowded diner, the bustle on the street outside reflective of the scene inside.

"Tyler, I can't even get the Hate Crimes Unit to admit they're working this case —"

"There's your proof."

"Proof of what!" Mimi snapped. "I don't even know what I'm looking for."

"You're looking for who's killing gay people."

"That's not my job! There's an extremely competent, not to mention extremely gorgeous, police Lieutenant whose job it is to find murderers."

Tyler said very quietly, "Don't you care?"

"Of course I care," she said wearily. "But the more I dig into this case, the more I find that what I want to know is why. I want to know how it happens that a person hates enough to kill."

Tyler picked up the menu, put it down again, drummed his fingers on the table, and played with the silverware. Mimi recognized the signals and waited for him to speak.

"People hate Blacks enough to kill ..." He spoke quietly, hesitantly. She nodded and he continued. "Do you understand that?"

"I think with racial hatred people can see what it is they fear, it becomes tangible ..." She'd never before articulated these thoughts and she paused to listen to herself. She always knew when her presence as a Black or as a woman was unwelcome — in a store or a restaurant or in an interview situation. But she never, ever worried about anyone's reaction to her sexual preference because nobody knew. . . . A feeling of horror spread through her.

"Tyler, those people knew their murderer. I'm sure of it."

With absolute clarity she saw that if Elizabeth Grayson, Phillip Tancil, Joseph Murray and Antonio delValle were killed because they were gay, the killer knew more about them than did their own families. Those people had fiercely guarded their secret, yet somebody had known, and it was a somebody each of them had followed willingly or met in a dark parking lot, late at night, far from home. Mimi pushed back her chair and stood so abruptly that she jarred the table, spilling water and startling Tyler.

"Where are you going?" he asked, steadying the glasses.

"To the gym. I need to think."

By unspoken agreement, afternoons at the Washington Women's Gym belonged to the serious body builders, the heavy-duty pumpers of iron. Mimi did not belong in that category, but she'd put in enough afternoon hours to be accepted as dedicated and serious — the attributes most respected by the pros. It had been a couple of months since Mimi's last afternoon workout and she wondered idly what familiar faces she'd see as she strolled into the locker room to change.

The gym was a converted warehouse and perfectly suited to its new function. It had high ceilings with high windows in which hung dozens of baskets of plants, and yards of open floor space which the owners had wisely partitioned into upper body, lower body, and free weight workout areas, with mirrors covering every wall and a warm, deep cranberry carpet on the floor. The aerobic area — rows of stair climbers, life cycles and treadmills — was adjacent to rows of mats for stretches, abdominals and other floor exercises. Energetic but not frantic disco music emanated at acceptable decibels from half a dozen speakers hung at intervals from the ceiling.

Mimi ran a quick mile on the treadmill then had lowered herself to a mat for stretches when a reflection in the mirror grabbed her attention: A back, not naked this time, the muscles fully flexed in a lateral pull down exercise. She watched transfixed as the muscles rippled and rolled under the olive skin, slowly, easily, again and again. Mimi wondered what it would feel like to have that power moving under her, on top of her . . .

Gianna completed her set, released the bar, and turned toward the upright rowing machine. She spied Mimi coming toward her and lifted a hand in greeting, crossing to meet her. Mimi was mesmerized by the fluidity of the lithe, graceful body that in repose offered no hint of the muscle power she'd just witnessed.

"It seems we're both cheating the system today," Gianna said in the familiar low voice.

"The system deserves it," Mimi said wryly and pulled on her weightlifting gloves. "Are you an afternoon regular?"

"A couple of times a week," Gianna said.

Mimi again appraised the body before her and

said with honest respect, "You don't get that body with a twice a week workout."

"Oh, I work out daily in the gym at headquarters. It's just that there are days when that's more of a hassle than I can handle and I appreciate the privacy and tranquility of this place."

"I can imagine," Mimi said with feeling, and she could. She wouldn't spend fifteen minutes in a leotard in a room with any of the cops she knew, and that included those she thought were nice guys. "You must have to wear sackcloth."

Gianna laughed and took a step away. "Let's get to it, shall we? I'll be watching your form, Miss Patterson."

They worked out in companionable silence though, true to her promise, Gianna watched her and Mimi was fully aware of it. She did not find the scrutiny uncomfortable but she was annoyed that she was unable to read any meaning into the glances. Idle curiosity, or attraction? Gianna never once dropped her veneer of cool, professional control, never gave away a hint of reaction. Mimi, on the other hand, seemed powerless to manage her responses to the other woman. While helping Gianna with her bench presses, Mimi was acutely conscious of the rapid breathing, of the tiny droplets of perspiration on her forehead and above her lip, of the light groans that escaped her throat with the effort of raising and lowering the one hundred and twenty-five pounds of weight. The breathing and the moisture and the sounds made Mimi think of other forms of exertion, and with those thoughts her nipples showed rock-hard through the thin Spandex of her workout bra. Gianna, if she noticed, remained impassive. Aggravated, Mimi stayed away from her until they were in the steam room together, stretched out full, Mimi on the bench above Gianna, the wet heat a soothing balm to their fatigued muscles.

"Seen Beverly lately?" Mimi asked idly.

"We had dinner together last night."

Gianna had responded just as idly and, Mimi thought, with just a hint of a smile. It wasn't the answer Mimi had expected and she was silent for a moment as she decided whether to ask a follow-up question.

"It seems you two are pretty close."

"We are," Gianna said with such ease that Mimi shut up and gave herself over to the soothing power of the steam. She was almost asleep when Gianna asked, "What does the 'M' stand for and do you use that byline to deliberately confound the unsuspecting?"

"Marilyn and yes." Mimi smiled. She could have used the byline Marilyn M. Patterson or even Mimi Patterson, but the ambiguity of M. Montgomery gave her an upper hand from which some of her subjects never recovered.

"Is it a family name?"

"I was named for my mother, for which I'll always be grateful. She died when I was seventeen, and I've always felt that having her name meant I was somehow living for her, too."

Silence hung in the steamy mist between them. Mimi felt no need to break it with small talk, nor, apparently did Gianna. Mimi knew they both were women whose entire days were filled with the thoughts, feelings, problems of others and they valued their moments of silent privacy, of pure, deep relaxation. They'd mastered the art of separating mind from body which is why, when needing to think, both escaped to the gym for a physical workout. Now, as her body luxuriated in the heat, her mind was a whirlwind of activity: she thought about the case, about how she could discuss it without damaging the fragile bond between them. And she thought about the growing power of the attraction between them.

Gianna stirred and Mimi said, "Gianna, would you...." just as the door opened to admit a group of laughing, talking body builders. The mood broken, Mimi and Gianna rose together, as if on cue, exchanged pleasantries with the new arrivals, and left the steam room.

Since their lockers were on opposite sides of the room and since there were now a half dozen or so other women present, they showered and dressed without speaking again. When Mimi turned to find Gianna, to say good-bye, she laughed, unable to stop herself. They were dressed almost exactly alike, the difference being only the color of their wardrobes. Mimi wore black wool slacks and a black blazer with a cranberry boat-neck sweater. Gianna wore moss green wool slacks and a matching blazer with a mustard colored boat-neck sweater, and she, too, laughed at their sameness.

She walked over to Mimi, pins sticking out of her mouth, hands busy in the dark mane of her hair as she tried to force it into submission.

"You started to say to me, 'Gianna would you...'

and you were interrupted. Maybe you could complete your sentence?"

Mimi looked into her eyes and said, "Would you let your hair just . . . be free?"

At Gianna's look of astonishment, Mimi apologized quickly. "I'm sorry. I had no right to say that."

Gianna didn't speak. She merely began to remove the pins from her hair, holding Mimi with her eyes, until the mass of rich, dark hair was spread out on her shoulders. They held each other's gaze. Then a beeper went off, and when they both checked their belts to see whose it was, Mimi realized she hadn't been breathing.

"It's yours," she said huskily to Gianna.

"No matter how much you cheat it, the system always wins," Gianna said, and she went to her locker, slammed it shut, took up her purse, and hurried away without looking back.

Mimi watched her leave, thinking again, *We are the same height and, I know, a perfect fit.*

The FBI had located Susan Jolley and had, that morning, returned her to Washington and to the custody of the Metropolitan Police. She'd been hiding out on one of the islands off the coast of South Carolina, which normally would have been a great place to hide. In the fall of the year, there is not much crime in coastal South Carolina, because all of the tourists are gone and the locals are too relieved at their departure to feel like raising hell. But the entire police force of that tiny island consisted of one retired FBI agent who made it his business to keep up with the Bureau's business — and Susan Jolley was the Bureau's business. Which was how that single law enforcement official came to have time to read every single FBI bulletin, and how Susan Jolley came to be, with her attorney, in an interview room waiting for Gianna, who scrutinized them through a two-way mirror.

Could this woman have murdered Liz Grayson? Or Phil Tancil or Tony delValle or Joe Murray? She was small and pale and she sat at the table, head down, long blonde hair obscuring her face, hands stretched out and clenched. The attorney whispered a few words to her and Susan Jolley raised her head, giving Gianna her first look at a face etched with pain and misery, at pale blue eyes hollowed out by lack of sleep, at thin lips compressed into a tight white line as if to keep locked inside the screams that lurked at the edge awaiting their chance to escape. She wore a flowered skirt and a pink T-shirt, no doubt adequate for the South Carolina coast but certainly insufficient protection for early November in Washington. She was, Gianna guessed, not more than thirty-five.

Gianna pushed open the door and entered the room quickly, crossing to introduce herself to the attorney. She sat down close to Susan Jolley and the woman shrank back into her chair. Gianna observed her closely for a moment, then began the questioning in her low, commanding voice.

"Miss Jolley, did you kill Elizabeth Grayson?"

"No," said Susan Jolley almost inaudibly, shaking her head.

"Do you know who killed Elizabeth Grayson?"

Again, the shake of the head and the little-voice "No."

"Did Karen Sachs kill Elizabeth Grayson?"

At that name, Susan Jolley recoiled from Gianna, twisting toward the lawyer, a plea on her face, her voice a series of little whimpers. The lawyer looked at Gianna, who kept her eyes on Susan Jolley.

"Why did you run away, Miss Jolley? Were you afraid that Karen Sachs had done something terrible, something to implicate you?"

Susan Jolley's resolve broke and she dropped her head on the table and sobbed. After a while, Gianna was able to extract her story. Susan Jolley and Elizabeth Grayson had quite literally bumped into each other in the lesbian literature section of Lammas Books at DuPont Circle on a Saturday afternoon. They'd talked and made suggestions to each other about which books to buy, and left the store together to have a cup of coffee.

Susan had fallen in love with Liz almost immediately. They met for lunch almost daily, and several times a week at Susan's house for dinner. And for lovemaking. At some point during the blossoming of her association with Liz, Susan broke off her affair with Karen Sachs.

"She hated Liz, blamed Liz, and it wasn't her fault," Susan sobbed. "It was my fault. I didn't love Karen, had never loved her, but I'd never said those words to Karen. So she thought Liz was the reason . . ."

"Did she threaten to kill Liz?" Gianna asked.

Susan sobbed helplessly. "Yes."

Gianna glanced at the attorney, expecting the

woman at this point to stop her client from talking. This was dangerous ground for the guilty. The attorney's face showed no sign of concern.

"And when you learned Liz had been murdered, you thought Karen did it?" Gianna waited. "Why, Susan, did you think that?" Because, Susan explained through her tears, Karen had a violent temper, had spied on Susan and Liz, had followed Liz home one night, had called Liz's home and raged at her husband, had vandalized her car.

Gianna spoke slowly, quietly. "Did Karen ever do anything to you, Susan? Did you ever see her engage in actual violence?"

"Only afterward," Susan replied, drying her eyes, calming herself. Gianna looked at Susan and saw someone who had now weathered the storm and emerged unscathed. Gianna had seen lots of worried lawyers and guilty clients and she saw neither here: the lawyer was relaxed and the client in mourning for the loss of a loved one.

"After what, Susan?" Gianna experienced the let-down cops get in the instant they realize their suspect didn't do it.

"After Liz left me and I wouldn't go back to her. Back to Karen, I mean. She didn't understand why I wouldn't . . ."

Gianna sagged as her only hope of a lead faded. She listened distractedly as Susan explained how Liz grew tired of Karen's threats and even more tired of Susan's pleas for them to spend more time together.

Bleak as Gianna felt about the case, however, Susan's next words stirred painful memories within her.

"Liz could never spend the night with me. She always had to go home to her husband and children. I thought...if she loved me...how could she not want to be with me?" Showing the first sign of animation, Susan continued. "She belonged to some group — women like her, gay but married — and they supported her position, said she had a right to have him and me. But I couldn't bear the thought of her making love with me, then rushing home to him! I'd be lying there, still burning from her and needing more, and she'd be gone home to him!"

Gianna knew that feeling so well. Too well. She forced those memories away and turned her attention back to Susan. "Why did you run away, Susan?"

"I had no more reason to be there," she said simply.

Gianna sat in the Hate Crimes team Think Tank surrounded by seven spirited faces. Uncharacteristically relaxed, her feet up on the desk, hands folded behind her head, Gianna let her mind wander as she listened to them talk. They were an exceedingly bright group of young police officers, all of whom had volunteered for this unit. They were Black and Asian and Hispanic and white, male and female, straight and gay, and she took a proprietary pride in them. She liked listening to them talk because they spurred her own thoughts and theories and because she always learned something.

"She was never my favorite suspect."

"Mine either. I was rooting for Karen. What a bi..."

"Careful, careful! That's no way to treat the public."

"Anyway. It's not a woman's crime. Women don't shoot people in the genitals, especially not another woman."

"That's a sexist remark! Besides, unfortunately, women get more like men every day."

"Talk about sexist remarks!"

"Anyway, it can't be Susan and Karen."

"Explain please?"

"They'd have a motive for Elizabeth Grayson only. That means we'd still be looking for who killed the three dudes."

"No shit Sherlock!"

"It scares me that there's somebody that crazy out there."

"It scares me that he — that whoever it is — would kill me just because I'm gay."

Gianna smiled inwardly at the ease with which they accepted and discussed their sexuality, their religion, their politics. She knew which of them were gay — she'd needed to in order to construct a balanced unit, and she needed several of them to be gay in order to conduct some kinds of undercover work.

She pushed their conversation to the back of her consciousness so she could think about where their next suspect might come from. She hadn't really believed that Susan Jolley was a serious candidate, not after reviewing her Army employment records, but Susan had been all they had and despite her probable innocence staring them in the face, there lingered a faint hope that something would come from her arrest. So now . . . the next course of action.

She flipped through Eric's report, frowning slightly. "You turning up anything in the groups and organizations?"

Eric shrugged and raised his palms heavenward. "We're inside a dozen of them, Anna, but you know how long it takes. I swear to God, as protective as some of these people are you'd think it was the nineteen-fifties all over again. The first time you ask a question about somebody they all get paranoid."

"Surely you're not surprised?" Cassandra Ali's tone was as arch as her eyebrows. "People still get fired or not hired at all for being queer. And besides, Detective, let's face it: you just don't look macho-butch enough to be totally believable in some of the places you've been frequenting lately."

The room exploded into laughter. Eric blushed deeply but took his ribbing good-naturedly, making a swaggering bow to Cassandra, who curtsied prissily in return.

They spent the next several hours reviewing the case, line-by-line, report-by-report. Gianna had questioned and pushed and probed until she was convinced that every angle had been covered and uncovered, and that every member of the team was familiar with every aspect of every file.

Finally, wearily, Gianna conceded, "Our only decent lead tells us that all four victims sought some kind of counseling for gay people. We'll focus on those that provide advice and help to people in the closet. Show the photographs around, drop the names. Somebody knew those people."

"But that could make a lot of people nervous," Kenny Chang said, "especially the killer. If that's where the killer finds his victims."

Kenny was one of a tiny handful of Chinese-Americans in the Department, and Gianna took it as a high compliment that he had abandoned the middle echelon of the elite Criminal Intelligence Division to work Hate Crimes. That he was about ten years older than the other team members, and therefore had that much more experience, also was a major plus.

"I want him nervous," Gianna said fervently. "I want him to think we're getting close. Maybe he'll make a mistake. Somewhere out there is a link to those four dead people, and I sure as hell want to find out who it is in the next two weeks." She did not need to remind them that in fourteen days it would be the 21st of November and that if history was destined to repeat itself, the fifth victim of a homosexual-hating monster would appear in a parking lot somewhere in the Nation's capital shortly after midnight.

She again leafed through the list of counseling and referral services, counting them and noticing that every one of her people was asleep standing up. She was about to assign herself to cover part of the list when the scowling visage of Captain Davis inserted itself into the doorway.

"What's this I hear about you cancelling a speech to the B'nai B'rith? And where the hell is that report comparing race crimes in D.C., Maryland and Virginia? I need that stuff for a speech I have to give to the National Council of Negro Women. Dammit, Anna, you promised! You can't let your duties slip!"

And he was gone as quickly as he appeared, leaving in his wake a greater dose of anger, confusion, dismay, and guilt. Gianna sighed and closed Eric's report and gathered all the files into a neat stack and put it on the floor, next to another stack of reports which she picked up and placed on the desk. She swiveled around in the chair and switched on the computer. She gave the screen her full attention as Eric led the others from the office.

Mimi walked up the steps of the sprawling Metropolitan Gay and Lesbian Community Organization thinking that it was the first such organizational contact she'd had since college when she'd regularly attended Gay Activist Alliance meetings — back when GAA was on the FBI list of dangerous and radical organizations; back when her own family would have viewed her emerging sexuality as dangerous and radical.

She felt energized now as she blended in with the stream of people milling about in the building's lobby which, with its red-and-green tiled floor, acoustical ceiling and gleaming oak doors and stair railings, still looked and felt just like a school. She saw a microcosm of the city's population: men and women of every age and color; well-dressed affluence and down right grubbiness; women with children; people with AIDS. Metro GALCO certainly lived up to its promise of serving the entire gay and lesbian community of the metropolitan Washington, D.C. area.

Once inside, Mimi took one look at the bulletin board and the schedule of activities and understood why Metro GALCO needed the old elementary school building for its headquarters. Every night of the week featured dozens of meetings, social gatherings, many sponsored by recognized and established organizations such as GLAAD, GAA, ACT UP, NOW, MADD, AA, NA, even an H & R Block Tax Preparation Seminar. There were dance classes, language classes, yoga classes, acting classes, writing classes, poetry readings. Looking at the bulletin board, and looking at the people surrounding her, Mimi realized with a warm feeling that being gay no longer had to mean being alone and isolated. But the warmth of that thought was quickly mitigated by the realization that somewhere in the building was someone who could help her understand why four people who had chosen to remain in the closet were now dead. Maybe someone in this building actually hated gay people, instead of loving them.

Scrutinizing the schedule of organizations and meetings, she focused on a series of lectures entitled *Out of the Closet and into the World,* and *Hi Honey, I'm Gay: Telling Your Spouse the Truth,* both facilitated by a Professor Calvin Cobbs. As she was writing days and times in her appointment book — and thinking that "facilitated" was a silly sounding word — she was joined by two young women who forthrightly and happily introduced themselves as Trisha and Mavis and who asked if she was on her way to the Cruise Room.

"To the, ah, what?" Mimi asked in confusion.

"That's just what we call it, jokingly," said Trish, tall and chocolate and gorgeous with a head full of baby dreadlocks and wearing a pair of skin tight jeans with more holes than Swiss cheese.

Mimi looked from the wide-open innocent eyes to the combat-booted feet and back again and forgot where she was and why. "Ah, call what?" she asked, struggling for equilibrium.

"The weekly get acquainted dance for women," said Mavis, with the slightest tinge of impatience. Her raven-black hair was cut impossibly short, her eyes were impossibly blue, the flash of smile much too seductive.

"There are sometimes some really nice women there," said Trish, with a complete and unabashed appraisal of Mimi, who laughed to herself at the notion of being cruised by a couple of kids whose combined ages she probably exceeded.

"Well?" said Mavis, hands on deliciously curving young hips, hugged by those deliciously tight jeans. "You coming?"

"You can dance, can't you?" asked Trish with that smile.

"Of course I can dance," said Mimi with the proper amount of attitude. "Let's go." And as she followed them, delighting in their youthful beauty and reminding herself that she had a niece their age, she marveled at how quickly the world had changed. Not only was it okay to be out of the closet at fifteen or sixteen, there was also a safe place to be once you emerged. Then she was struck by another thought, one that sapped a bit of the swagger from her step: the world had changed so much that all the dances she knew belonged to another time. . . .

VI

"What in the ever-lovin' bloody hell is the FBI doing poking around in my case?" Gianna stopped pacing long enough to throw the file she held across the room. "Goddammit, somebody better have an answer for me!"

Gianna's team looked at her in wide-eyed amazement. Eric attempted a hesitant response. "Well, they did find Susan Jolley..."

Gianna stopped him cold. "That doesn't give them the right to access my case files. I want to know who this 'Don' person is and why he wants the files on this case!"

Eric tried again. "It seems to be a personal matter, Anna, ah, Lieutenant..."

She smiled bleakly, reached to Eric and squeezed his arm. That simple, personal action seemed to release all the tension in the room.

"Don't you 'Lieutenant' me, Detective. Listen, guys. I'm pretty damn certain that what we're searching for is in those files and I don't want anybody outside this unit messing around in them, especially some dipshit FBI guy. Everybody clear about that?"

There was a general murmuring of assent.

"Do you really think we're looking at the answer and just not seeing it?" asked Linda Lopez, another veteran who'd jumped ship from Fraud to join Hate Crimes. Detail was Linda's strong suit and Gianna knew that she loved burying herself in facts and figures and finding the one that didn't belong.

"I do," Gianna said emphatically, "and Linda, I want you and Kenny to turn these files sideways. We know there's one common link between these four people and that's some kind of gay counseling. But we've got to make it more specific..." And there *was* something, Gianna was sure of it. "Cassie, how're you coming on the nationwide check of homicides on the twenty-first of the month for the last five years?"

Cassie groaned and buried her head in her hands. "Do you know how many people have been killed on the twenty-first, especially when the moon was full?"

Gianna laughed out loud. "The other part of the equation, Cassie, was that the victim or the perp was gay or there was even the hint of gay, not that the moon was full."

"I'm on it, I'm on it," Cassie groaned loudly.

"You still think he's marking some kind of anniversary, that the murders are ritualistic?" asked Kenny Chang.

"It's one of the few theories I've got left that makes any sense at all," Gianna said with a shrug, and almost immediately those words pushed to the surface a thought, a feeling, something that had nagged at her for days, one of those things that would never quite take shape on its own but with the proper impetus bloomed fully.

"The parking lots. Why those parking lots? We need to make the connection between the victims and the location they were found."

"You seem certain there is one," Eric said.

"These are logical crimes, people. The logic may be a bit cracked but it's there. There's nothing random or haphazard or accidental about any of this."

Tyler and Mimi huddled in the hallway behind the newsroom near the recycling bin, the only really private place in the newsroom, and she was almost enjoying his discomfort as she pressed him for more details about his association with Phil Tancil.

"Right now, you're my best lead, Tyler," she pleaded.

And he was. Tancil's wife had become hysterical,

screaming when Mimi introduced herself as a
reporter, throwing the rake she'd been using on the
yard, missing Mimi's head by mere inches. Joe
Murray's wife had refused to open the door, and
Tony delValle's wife threatened to sue for libel,
slander, defamation of character, and everything else
she could think of if Mimi persisted in asking
questions about her dead husband. Elizabeth
Grayson's former house was empty, a For Sale sign
in the front yard. The neighbors either didn't know
or wouldn't say where the family had gone.

"That leaves you, Tyler. You knew the man. He's
dead. Murdered. Tell me something. Anything!"

Tyler shook his head in misery. Mimi wasn't sure
whether he was telling her no or whether he was
finally buckling, finally caving in. Mercilessly, she
shot her final arrow. "He was your friend, Tyler. You
owe him this much."

The arrow hit home. Forty-four year old Phillip
Tancil had been Mr. Middle America. Born in
Baltimore, college at Georgetown, MBA at Wharton,
back to D.C. to a job offer at a bank, a fast and
accomplished rise to the top. He'd had sexual
encounters with men beginning at age sixteen, but
in graduate school he'd found himself attracted to a
woman classmate, had given thanks and married her
quickly and became as successful at being a husband
and father as he was a banker. But no matter how
roomy the closet, the attraction to one's own sex is a
powerful pull and being a white collar, corporate
American success hadn't made Phil Tancil any less
susceptible to the pull. He soon established a
separate life, a group of friends separate from the
friends he shared with his wife, men with whom he

played golf and tennis and poker. Men with whom he was free to be his true self. Men like himself — successful corporate men with whom he could have sex without endangering his home life.

"Any of those other men married, Tyler?" Mimi asked.

"Yeah," Tyler said warily. "Why?"

"I need to talk to them..."

"No way! Those are my friends, Mimi."

"Phil Tancil is your *dead* friend, Tyler," Mimi hissed, dimly aware that one or two people had crossed to the recycling bin during their conversation. Looking dejected, Tyler ran his fingers through his hair.

"Tyler, did Phil belong to any groups, you know, the gay groups that help people work through their problems?"

"Yeah," Tyler said, removing his glasses and squeezing his temples. "Some kind of counseling thing for married people. It made him feel better because they didn't tell him he was a jerk for deceiving his wife. He told me once he felt like enough of a creep without paying somebody to tell him he was."

"The name of this counseling group. Do you —"

"I don't know," he said wearily, "I'll ask around. Maybe one of the guys will remember. One of the married ones..." He trailed off, obviously distressed. Mimi sympathized with his dilemma though she was still annoyed by his stony unwillingness to push his friends for information and she told him as much.

He didn't appreciate her forthrightness. "I didn't expect you to badger me like you do your scuzzy politicians, Patterson," he snarled at her. Oddly enough his words and his tone hurt and she wilted and retreated. "Why did you put me on this story, Tyler? Because I'm gay?"

"Because you care about right and wrong, Patterson. Because you hate it when people suffer unnecessarily. Because you're one pushy broad. I'm going home. See you Monday."

Mimi walked slowly back to her desk drained, depressed, and with an overwhelming sense of uselessness. Two weeks of work and not a single lead, not one scrap of new information, and not the slightest idea how to proceed. She looked around the almost empty newsroom and wondered if she, too, should pack it in for the weekend and start fresh on Monday. Her phone rang and she looked up at the wall of clocks, frowning.

"Yes?"

"Ciao, Mimi. Io sono Gianna. Come sta?"

Mimi stuttered in surprised confusion, both at hearing Gianna's voice so unexpectedly and at hearing her speak Italian.

"Ah, Gianna . . . ah, molto bene . . ." Every word of Italian she knew had fled her brain, leaving her stumbling like a first-time tourist.

"I'm making a big assumption that since you're still at work you haven't eaten and I've just made a pot of vegetarian chili and a big salad and I wondered if you'd care to join me for dinner?"

"How," Mimi asked carefully, "did you know I'm a vegetarian?"

"Bev told me," Gianna said breezily. "So, are you coming?"

"Ah," Mimi cleared her throat, "what's the address?" She wrote down an address just over the

77

Maryland line in Silver Spring not far from her own upper northwest D.C. house.

She stored her files and tried to make some order out of the chaos on her desk, but her mind was spinning. Why this out-of-the-blue dinner invitation at nine o'clock on a Friday night, and what the hell is she doing talking to Beverly about me?

When she got off the elevator on the fourteenth floor of the aging but elegant pre-war building, the aromas of several dinners wafting out into the hallway from behind closed doors bombarded her, and she realized how hungry she was. Still irritated, but very hungry, she pressed the door bell.

Gianna opened the door immediately and surprised Mimi with a brief but warm hug and ushered her into a warmly elegant room. She expressed delight that Mimi had stopped to get her flowers and spent a few moments arranging them, moments during which Mimi had time to survey her surroundings, beginning with Gianna. She wore black tights and a white shirt and her hair was loose and wild. Fresh flowers were everywhere and Mimi was glad she'd decided to take the time to get them. Gianna clearly loved them.

Framed photographs shared every surface with the vases of flowers — photographs of people young and old, all of whom resembled Gianna enough for Mimi to assume they were family; and one in particular — a striking woman whose loose, wild hair had turned to silver and who Mimi would bet was Gianna's mother.

Done with the flowers, Gianna was now pouring wine — Mimi's favorite Chianti. The anger that had dissipated swiftly returned. "Is this an accident or did you know I liked this wine?"

"Of course it's not an accident. Bev told me —"

"And what the hell else did Bev tell you?"

"Well, obviously," Gianna said with calculated calm, "she told me where to find you since you weren't at home."

"Anything else?" Mimi said coldly.

"No," said Gianna calmly. "The other thing I want to know I'll find out for myself. Shall we eat?"

Mimi shrugged in good-natured defeat and helped Gianna carry the food to the table, an antique, battered pine polished to a high gloss, the kind upon which every meal was served in every town and village in Southern Italy. The vegetarian chili notwithstanding, it was a very Italian meal — hot and toasty foccaccio, tomatoes and bufala mozzarella, spinach sauteed in garlic and pignolis, and crisp green salad. Mimi laughed with delight as she sat down. Italian hospitality and food were always so wonderful and always so much, too much.

"*E piu di abbastanza,*" she said to Gianna, who laughed a full, golden, throaty laugh.

"Your accent needs a little work, but I get the message. How did you learn to love things Italian?"

"It's so easy," Mimi said softly, watching the candlelight dance and reflect in Gianna's eyes, and as the color crept into Gianna's face she lowered her eyes and they ate in silence for a few moments.

"You must think me an awful glutton," Mimi said, remembering but not caring that she was talking with her mouth full. "I know I've eaten recently, I just don't remember when it was."

"I am truly relieved to know that there are

people who work worse hours and have worse eating habits than cops!"

They chatted easily throughout the meal, through the excellent espresso, as they cleared the table and cleaned the kitchen and settled into the luxurious claret-colored couch to talk even more: about football (Mimi as a Redskins fan, Gianna as an Eagles fan); about religion; about politics; about art; about film. Gianna was relaxed and entertaining, bearing no resemblance to the calm and controlled Lieutenant Maglione. And they were both aware of their efforts to keep the conversation clear of work — clear of any subject that would lead them to the four murders.

"I'm sorry I snapped at you earlier. You didn't deserve that. I guess I'm a little touchy..."

"Relationships are touchy things." Gianna looked distant.

"Anyway," Mimi said quickly to bring her back, "you said there was something you wanted to know, something you'd find out for yourself. Well, ask away. You've guaranteed my cooperation with your hospitality."

"Really?" said Gianna almost under her breath as she took Mimi's glass and placed it on the kidney-shaped coffee table. Then she leaned toward Mimi. "I want to know what it's like to make love with you but I don't want to hear about it from somebody else."

Mimi reached out to Gianna, to touch, to savor the silky, dark richness of her hair. Slowly, gently, she ran her fingers through it until she held the back of Gianna's neck and drew her in close, closer, until their lips touched, softly, briefly, and then — then the fire of arousal that had smoldered within

80

her for so many weeks, burst into full flame. The soft fullness of Gianna's lips released the surging electricity transmitted by her searching, probing tongue. Mimi pulled away to breathe, to look into Gianna's eyes, to confirm reality.

Gianna stood abruptly, pulling Mimi up with her. "Come on." They undressed en route to the bedroom, hasty like teenagers, leaving a trail of clothes, and Mimi laughed lightly when she saw the all-white bed ensemble.

"What?" Gianna whispered.

"You'll see," Mimi breathed, pulling Gianna into the bed and onto her body and almost crying out at the perfection of her. She caressed her fully, finger tips exploring, searching, learning, matching the rhythm of their tongues. Gianna seemed not to breathe. Mimi turned her over, to be on top, and Gianna's back arched and she pressed powerfully into Mimi. Mimi pulled her mouth from Gianna's and began with her mouth and tongue the exploration already made by her fingers. She gently bit her neck and along her collarbone on both sides and the breath that had been caught in Gianna's throat escaped in a little cry that became a louder cry when Mimi teased and teased and teased and then took gently between her teeth first one nipple and then the other. And as she brought her mouth, her tongue back to Gianna's mouth, her hand caressed slowly and inexorably down the firm, muscled belly to rich, dark, luxurious hair and gently and slowly fingers parted and searched and found and the gentle, slow, oh so slow, touching began. And continued. Forever. And there was Mimi's kiss, urgent, tense, tongue demanding, and then her teeth and tongue again urging her nipples to erection and all the time the soft, slow touching between her legs until Gianna could no longer stand it.

"Mimi," she whispered with rasping breath, and Mimi took her mouth from the exquisite breast and brought her ear to Gianna's mouth and Gianna whispered to her and even as the breathless words escaped Mimi was obeying, her fingers being received into the deep, wet, warmth. Received and locked in and the touching was no longer soft but strong and surging and Gianna arched to meet her. Mimi encircled her waist with her free arm and Gianna wrapped her arms around Mimi's shoulders and with every surge of the fingers she whispered, "Yes" until it was no longer a whisper and Mimi listened and felt and timed her fingers to the cries until they stopped and the body-racking shudders began. And then she wrapped her arms and legs around Gianna and kissed the tears from her face.

Gianna stirred and stretched her body the length of Mimi's and opened her eyes and looked into dark, liquid pools.

"You've been watching me," Gianna whispered.

"Um hum." Mimi smiled, continued to probe with her eyes.

"What?" Gianna traced Mimi's lips with her tongue before she allowed her to answer.

"How long . . . how long since . . ."

Gianna groaned and buried her face in Mimi's

shoulder, her response a muffled protest. "Oh, God, don't ask me that, Mimi, please. Don't ask me . . ."

"I want to know, Gianna." She lifted Gianna's head from her shoulder, holding her face in her hands, and looked into eyes liquid with tears. "Oh, baby," she breathed, kissing away her tears for the second time. "I didn't mean for the question to hurt you. I'm so sorry . . ."

Gianna shook her head free of Mimi's hands and said defiantly, "Almost two years and I know that probably sounds ridiculous and dumb to you, that a normal, sane woman would go almost two years without sex!"

"Well, maybe it is a bit worse than a normal, sane woman going one year, three months, and seventeen days without sex." Mimi tried a little laugh that didn't quite work but it didn't matter because Gianna had rolled her over and climbed on top of her and burned her mouth with a kiss so intense Mimi thought she'd die from it. Then Gianna began to move on her, a rhythm so subtle, so faint, she wasn't sure it was real until the heat in her mouth spread to her breasts and to her legs and she groaned and wrapped her legs around Gianna's waist and Gianna's mouth released Mimi's lips and went to Mimi's ear and she whispered and Mimi groaned again and breathed "Yes . . . yes . . . please . . ." And still Gianna whispered . . .

Mimi held Gianna's hair as if that would help her withstand the passion coursing through her body. Gianna had teased every inch of her with her mouth, stopping no one place very long but returning again and again to her breasts to lick, nip, suck, and then on to another spot and then again and again to the moist, hot triangle where her tongue would dart in and out and in and out and then move on to some other place until finally, on one such foray, Mimi held her head there, to force her to please ... And Gianna took one of Mimi's wrists in each of her hands and she slid herself up the length of Mimi's body and kissed her mouth so softly and gently, her tongue so sweet, that Mimi wanted to cry and then Gianna whispered to her again and Mimi was unable to speak because she knew that Gianna's slide back down her body would finally, blessedly, give her what was promised.... Yes.... Now.... Mimi cried out as Gianna's tongue quickly sought and found the place and explored and found all the places, and the hands that had gripped her wrists now opened and intertwined her fingers and Mimi held on as powerful release tensed and arched her body and eventually ebbed. She sighed. And then the tongue, like a lightning rod, sought and found the place again and again the storm gathered and grew inside her and again it broke, great waves crashing within but now she knew from the throbbing that did not cease with the crashing waves that Gianna's tongue would find the place again ... and again ... Everything they knew about being women, about loving women, they shared with each other until the orange sun crept from behind the blue-bruised clouds and then they locked themselves into each other's arms and slept.

* * * * *

Mimi awoke disoriented but quickly placed herself and her surroundings and the deliciously warm body spooning her. But what was that incessant, high-pitched tone?

"What's that noise," she demanded with sleepy indignation.

"Your beeper," Gianna mumbled into Mimi's shoulder.

"How do you know it's mine," Mimi asked hopefully.

"Because mine is in the bedside table," Gianna mumbled again as Mimi reluctantly slid from beneath the covers, wrapping her arms around herself and shivering, following the demanding call of the beeper. "There are clothes all over the place," she called to Gianna from the hallway as she located her slacks with the beeper still attached to the belt and howling for attention.

"Wonder how that happened," Gianna remarked wryly and almost immediately paid for her impertinence when Mimi came leaping across the room and onto the bed. She pounced on Gianna, tickling and biting her ribcage, reducing her to breathless, shrieking laughter that quickly became breathless, shuddering moans when Mimi turned her attention — and her tongue — to nipples.

"Stop!" she moaned. "Mimi, stop!"

"Why," demanded Mimi, her tongue still active.

"Because you need to answer your bleeping beeper," Gianna groaned, pushing her away.

"Oh, hell," Mimi groused, looking at the digital display on the beeper, frowning as Gianna gave her the cellular telephone. Mimi punched in the numbers.

"Hi, it's me. What's up?" she said to Freddy Schuyler.

"Where are you? I've been calling you since last night! You have worried me half to death!"

"I'm sorry, Freddy, I didn't mean to worry you. I'm fine."

"Where are you?" Freddy demanded again.

"Never mind where I am, okay?"

"Not okay but no problem. Dinner's at eight . . ."

"Dinner?" asked Mimi mindlessly.

"Oh, you forgot! I'll bet I know what you've been doing! Well, who is she? Anyone I know?"

"No, Freddy. Good-bye. I'll see you at eight."

"Bring her. We can have a double engagement party."

"Good-bye, Freddy."

"Bring her, Mimi. I want to see what's left of the woman who had you after a year and a half of celibacy!"

"I'll ask her, okay? Now good-bye!" Mimi returned the phone to Gianna, turned to face her. "That was my friend, Freddy. I'm supposed to have dinner at his house tonight, to meet his new boyfriend, and you're invited, if you'd like to come."

"And what else did he say?" Gianna wore her half smile.

"What do you mean?"

"He said something and you blushed."

"I did not!" Mimi said hotly.

"You're doing it again." Gianna's smile grew as her light green-brown eyes bored into Mimi's dark brown ones. Mimi leaned closer to her and whispered in her ear and Gianna laughed a deep, throaty golden laugh that made Mimi tingle.

"Now, where was I before I was so rudely interrupted?"

"Right there," Gianna whispered, pulling back the covers and pointing to a fully aroused right nipple.

Mimi watched with amused amazement as Freddy melted before Gianna's charms. Of all the women she'd shared her life with he'd liked Beverly best, and had been really angry with her over their breakup. He'd actually agreed with Bev that until Mimi learned how to treat women, she should leave them alone. And now here he was practically genuflecting before Gianna. Probably, Mimi mused, because she praised his lasagna up one side and down the other and ate three servings. Vanity, thy name is gay boy!

Freddy's penthouse apartment and everything in it — furniture, art work, even plants — were scaled to offensive tackle size. The living room was thirty feet long with a wall of windows that all but brought the Potomac River inside. The fireplace was almost as huge as the one in his mountain cabin. The sofa, constructed so Freddy could lounge comfortably in it, swallowed normal adult beings whole, making them feel like children with their feet dangling off the floor. And the entire offensive line would feel right at home at the dining table. For all its massiveness, however, Freddy's home exuded warmth, thanks to a lighting design that always baffled Mimi because she could never find the lights, and to pastel colors of sand and lime and coral and other mixtures that, until witnessed, would never have been considered masculine.

Cedric served coffee and dessert — a pear torte he'd made himself and which was absolutely, sinfully delicious. Mimi studied him again for perhaps the sixth time that night, thinking that Freddy's loving description barely did the man justice. Cedric was almost as tall as Freddy, but much thinner: he had the runner's lean, lithe body compared to Freddy's bulk. Cedric was the color of a chocolate bar and had the voice of a nineteen-sixties doowop crooner: slow, deep and scratchy. Freddy had said Cedric was forty, but the mischievous eyes that crinkled behind the wire-rimmed glasses, the ready laugh that kept the dimples showing deep in his cheeks, made him look fifteen years younger.

Her joy for Freddy bubbled over. "With you both cooking like this, you'll have fat thighs and pot bellies in six months," Mimi teased.

"Ah, but what a way to go," sighed Freddy, smiling at Cedric, and Mimi noticed he'd looked at his watch again, the third time in the last forty-five minutes.

"If we've stayed too long, Freddy, just let me know. After all, I do have plans for Gianna and the fireplace," Mimi said.

Freddy laughed good-naturedly and reached for a second helping of the torte. "I'm sorry. You two are welcome to stay in our lives forever, though I know what a poor substitute we are for the fireplace."

"I think you two are swell, but this is the first I've heard of this fireplace, so pardon me if I'm intrigued." Gianna looked expectantly at Mimi. "Well?"

"Good things come to those who wait," Mimi chuckled, and turned to Freddy. "So, why the attention to time tonight?"

"It's nothing, Mimi, really . . ."

"Oh, tell them, Fred. These are your friends," urged Cedric.

"It's that outing business," Freddy said miserably.

"Oh, God, that's tonight!" Mimi exclaimed. "I'd forgotten!"

"What outing business? What are you talking about," Gianna asked, and as Freddy explained, a change overtook her that startled Mimi until she realized that it was the Lieutenant Maglione persona: the utter stillness, the intensity of her gaze, the low, controlled tones of her voice.

"And what do they plan to do, stand outside and tell everybody who goes in that you're gay?" Gianna was in a cold rage.

Freddy shrugged dejectedly, mumbled that they hadn't told him their plans, and looked at his watch again.

It was a little after ten, and for the next two hours the upwardly mobile and the already-arrived beautiful people from D.C. and the neighboring Maryland and Virginia suburbs would line up to pay their way into Schuyler's to hear, see and dance to the hottest reggae or jazz or rock in town; to shoot billiards upstairs; to eat hickory-smoked barbecue in the back room. By midnight the place would be packed and from that moment until the four a.m.

closing time, the place would pulse with fevered energy. And Freddy was always a welcoming, sporting presence, slapping high-fives with the football fans and gracefully receiving the adulation of the women who swooned in the presence of his handsome bulk. How would these people respond to the knowledge that their hero was gay?

"Would it really be so tragic, Fred, if you're out of the closet? I mean, if there's nothing to hide, there's nothing to reveal." Cedric spoke in the matter-of-fact tone typical of the British, sounding ever so reasonable.

Except to Freddy. "Why can't you understand? My private life is my private business! It's not a matter for public discussion."

"Do you actually believe your life will be the topic of discussion in the homes of Washington? I rather think there's a young boy somewhere, a soccer player or a baseball player or a long distance runner, who'll hear the news about Freddy Schuyler and know with relief that it's all right for him to feel what he feels deep inside himself."

"Cedric, I didn't ask to be anybody's role model," Freddy said wearily.

"That's what you are, Fred, whether you asked or not. Do you know how many kids — boys and girls — wear your number on their jerseys? You were an institution in this town for fifteen years."

"And now I'm just a guy who owns a restaurant."

"If you were just a guy who owned a restaurant there'd be nobody who cared whether you slept with me or your cow." Cedric's tone was a plea for Freddy to hear, to understand. "You're important to people,

Fred, and it's important that people know who and how and what you really are."

Mimi saw that Gianna was listening to the exchange with a similar degree of unease. Undoubtedly she also was thinking of the four murder victims, apparently dead because of their secret lives. And yet . . .

"But Cedric, doesn't Freddy, don't I, have a right to a private life?" Mimi reached across the table to touch Cedric's arm.

He took her hand. For the first time the little-kid light in his eyes dimmed and his deep voice went deeper, the clipped British accent becoming more pronounced. "You're talking about keeping secrets, Mimi. That's different from a private life. When you keep your sexuality a secret it suggests you're somehow ashamed of it, and it's that sense of shame that gives people who hate us their best and biggest weapon. If we all lived as if we didn't give a damn what anybody thought, pretty soon nobody would think about it at all. And who we love certainly wouldn't be a source of fear and danger."

Cedric gave Mimi's hand a gentle squeeze before releasing it and then he turned to Freddy and took his hand. "Come on, luv, let's drive over to the club and take a look, shall we?"

Gianna pushed back her chair and stood up. "I'm ready."

Mimi said, "Gianna and I will meet you there."

It was a short distance from Freddy's Georgetown waterfront penthouse apartment to the Adams-Morgan location of the club, but Saturday night traffic tripled the normal driving time, so there was ample opportunity for Mimi to bring Gianna up to date on her research on outing — every available newspaper article on the subject from New York to Los Angeles and everywhere in between: the not always congenial interview in the *Blade* with the guy from Queer Nation; the endless discussions with her own friends, most of whom shuddered at the thought of being forced out of the closet.

Mimi concluded, "But even those who hate the outers with a passion don't believe they kill people."

"They're lucky not to be victims themselves." Gianna spoke with such venom that Mimi turned to look at her and then had to slam on the brakes to keep from hitting the car in front of her in the bumper-to-bumper traffic snaking up 18th Street.

"I was in New York last year for a seminar and I was walking in Greenwich Village and I saw posters plastered all over, on walls and telephone stalls, photographs of actors and singers — big stars — and under the photos the words DEFINITELY QUEER and I remember being shocked, not that they were gay, but that somebody would expose them so ... so ... brutally." Gianna shook her head at the memory. "Do they say why they do it, Mimi? Did you ask why they do it?"

Mimi had asked one very vocal outer that exact question. His response still disturbed her: "Homosexuality is not a privacy issue." And Cedric's words reverberated in her head: "Keeping secrets is different from privacy." The concept whirled around and around in her brain until Gianna interrupted the process.

"I wouldn't have this job if the entire police department knew about me. Ironic and stupid as it is, there wouldn't be a Hate Crimes Unit if the people on the City Council who had to approve the money knew I was a lesbian. But according to the outers, the world would be a better place if everybody in it knew I made love with you? I'm sorry. I don't get it." Gianna snorted in disgust.

"Does the Chief know about you?" Mimi asked casually.

"Wouldn't surprise me. That old buzzard knows everything. He probably knows about you, too," Gianna said offhandedly, causing Mimi to stop short. The screech of brakes followed by a bellowing horn testified to the proximity of the car behind them.

"What do you mean he *probably* knows about me, too?"

"Well, he's always asking if we're getting along like he predicted we would — you've heard him yourself. Besides, your own editor knew about you so what are you so snippy about?"

Mimi heard the laugh beginning in Gianna's throat and sought to quell it. "He didn't know, he asked," she replied haughtily, and Gianna did laugh at her, running a hand up Mimi's thigh and causing her to swerve toward the adjacent lane.

"He asked because he knew, Mimi. Now pay attention to your driving. We're almost there."

They could see the crowd in front of Schuyler's from a block and a half away, a crowd, Mimi knew — though she was not yet close enough to see — was comprised of young women in skimpy, slinky dresses and spike heels and young men in full, Italian-cut suits. She could, however, see Freddy very clearly — bigger than everybody — walking up and down the line shaking hands. And then she could see a small knot of perhaps ten people, definitely not dressed for entry into Schuyler's, passing out flyers.

She whipped the Karmann Ghia into the lot and parked in a Reserved for Management spot next to Freddy's Ford Bronco, thinking the thing must be part helicopter to have arrived so far ahead of them. Gianna was out and aiming for the front door before Mimi could shut off the ignition and the lights. She trotted after her in intrigued pursuit.

"Do you have a permit for this demonstration?" Gianna demanded of the protesters.

"Who the hell are you?" snarled a belligerent young man with bleached blond hair and three earrings.

Gianna reached into her pocket, took out her ID, held it close to his face, and asked the same question again, only this time the voice was colder.

"Oink, oink," said another of the protesters.

"Somebody get him a Kleenex. Or a feed bag," said Gianna, and some of those lined up to get into Schuyler's snickered.

"Why don't you ask them for a permit," snarled the blond, pointing a thumb disdainfully to the line.

"They're in a line behind a rope which the establishment has a permit for —" But drowning out Gianna, one of the protestors yelled to the crowd, "Freddy Schuyler is a queer! A big, strong, football playing queer!"

And then they began to chant, "We're everywhere, we're everywhere!"

A man from the line rushed up to the protestors, a man built very much like Freddy, and grabbed the blond's shirt front. "I oughta break your face," he spat.

Gianna grabbed his wrist with the vise-like grip Mimi knew so well and propelled him back to the line and then she turned to the blond leading the protest.

"You people have three seconds to clear this sidewalk or I promise you, if I have to call for backup, you won't get out of jail until some time Monday. Late Monday. Your choice."

"Fucking fascist," muttered the blond.

"If I were a facist you wouldn't get a choice. Now beat it."

Reluctantly the demonstrators ambled off to the cheers, jeers and whistles from those in line. The men in line reached out to Freddy to shake his hand, to clap him on the back. The women reached up to plant kisses on his face. They either didn't hear, didn't understand, or didn't care about the message of the demonstration.

Mimi watched the protesters depart. Of the ten, only three of them — all men — had actually spoken. The others had joined in the "We're everywhere" group cheer but otherwise remained silent. Not, Mimi thought, reflective of what she knew about ACT UP or Queer Nation. Mimi noticed one woman in particular, short and rather dumpy, who looked at least fifty and had kept staring intently at Gianna. Who were these people?

She watched as they slouched away, slowly, grudgingly, and without a backward glance, led by the dumpy woman, not the aggressive blond. *Who the hell were they?* No activist group turns tail and runs just because the cops, to say nothing of a single, off-duty, out-of-uniform cop, gives an order.

Gianna was huddled with Freddy, away from the line, he leaning down low to hear her, both their faces intent and sober, Gianna doing most of the talking. Then Freddy straightened, wrapped Gianna in a bear hug, and she started to walk in Mimi's direction.

Taking her cue, Mimi turned and headed for the parking lot and noticed a pile of flyers from the fizzled demonstration strewn on the ground. She picked up one of the flyers, folded it, and tucked it into her purse. Gianna walked right past her to the parking lot, muttering *soto voce*, "Pick up another of those, would you?" And then Mimi shivered and realized that the night air was cold.

They didn't speak on the drive uptown to Mimi's house, didn't speak while Mimi built a roaring fire, didn't speak while Mimi laid a couple of quilts and big pillows on top of the rug, didn't speak until one of the big logs rolled off the grate, crackling and spitting fire and a spark jumped over the screen and onto the quilt and they both scrambled to put it out before it burned a hole.

Then, finally, Mimi said, "You know we're going to have to talk about it eventually."

It. The case, the horrible murders of the four gay people.

It. The thing that represented each woman's job and therefore the potential for major conflict between them given that the natural relationship between cops and press was adversarial at best and downright hostile in the worst case.

Gianna sighed a deep, weary sigh and said, "Can we do it tomorrow?"

And Mimi nodded. Tomorrow. Yes. So we can have this one more night of perfect, exquisite beauty before the ugliness intrudes.

And they devised new ways to pleasure each other until the once roaring blaze was only a smoldering memory and they ran naked and shrieking in the freezing air into the bedroom and Gianna laughed when she saw the all-white bed ensemble, laughed the throaty, golden laugh that gave Mimi the tingles and then they were under the covers . . .

VII

Tyler took off his glasses to look at Mimi across the table, as if seeing her differently would somehow minimize the horror of her words. His eyes blinked and his lips trembled and he squeezed the spoon as if trying to bend it in half. He waved away the waiter who approached to take their order, returned his glasses to his face.

As Mimi watched him she thought again how ridiculous it was for people to think about — talk about — expect — something loosely referred to as objectivity from reporters. Reporters were human beings and human beings responded the same way as anyone else to shock and horror. She remembered her own reaction when Gianna told her in graphic detail how the four people died and now she watched Tyler restore his face and his emotions to some kind of normal state.

"We have to report this," he said in a tight voice.

"We can't," Mimi said. "I won't, Tyler. I gave her my word that any information she shared with me at this point would be on deep background. I won't break my word."

Mimi was more adamant than she knew was necessary. Tyler would never expect a reporter to violate the sanctity of a source; but he was so horrified by what she had just told him that clear-eyed reason was not his initial response. Mimi understood completely, still not having recovered fully from the mind-numbing shock of learning how the four victims died. She looked more closely at Tyler, wondering how much of his reaction was due to the fact that someone he knew had died in such a monstrous manner, reminding herself that this was more than just a story for him.

"So what now," Tyler said listlessly.

"Back to Metro GALCO. That's my best hope for a lead."

"Why not the Nazis!" exclaimed Tyler bitterly.

"Because the killer is someone who was able to get close to those people, Tyler, somebody they knew and/or trusted. I don't think Nazis fall into that category, much as we might wish it."

"Do the police have any leads?" he asked, chastened.

"No," Mimi answered flatly.

She thought again of Gianna's face and voice and attitude as they discussed the case, and believed that Gianna had not lied when she said the police were at a dead end. She realized that of necessity Gianna hadn't told her everything the police knew about the murders; but she also felt that Gianna was leveling with her when she claimed the police had no leads, and she knew that fact terrified her, terrified them both, and saddened them, because what was growing between them could not take full flower until the murderer was caught — whenever that would be. Gianna had adamantly refused to even discuss the proposition that they work the case together.

"We don't do the same job, Mimi. Let's get that clear. There's nothing you can do to help me."

Mimi had been stung by Gianna's blunt dismissal of her suggestion, and by the fact that she could so quickly cease being Gianna the lover — passionate and insatiable — and become Anna Maglione, super cop, focused totally, completely, and only on the job at hand. *She's actually worse than I am,* Mimi was thinking as she was snatched into reality.

"What, Tyler? Did you say something?"

"I asked if you're all right."

"No. No, I'm not all right. And for the first time in my life that thought scares the shit out of me."

"Why now, Mimi?" Tyler asked, real concern in his voice.

"Because now I care about something other than the story. That's new for me and I don't know what to do with it."

She saw that Tyler knew what she meant and her respect for him increased several notches when he took his eyes from hers and focused all his attention on the menu.

Gianna saw in the faces looking up at her all the things she expected to see: rage, disbelief, horror, sadness, resignation. No matter what the group or organization, no matter what its purpose, no matter what the length of its involvement in trying to make the world a better place, people were never prepared for the truth of hate in America, and Gianna could always see it in the faces of the people. Black people, Hispanic people, Jewish people, gay people, people of all colors — all the people so familiar with hate. The faces of the B'nai B'rith of northwest Washington were no different.

She'd only been on the job and making these speeches for a short time, but she'd already formulated a theory about why her audience always seemed unprepared for the depth and extent of the hatred that permeated society: they must want to — need to — think that the people who did the hating all lived somewhere else. So when she recited the statistics for the seven jurisdictions that she monitored, and compared them with Washington, there was always shock. This was, after all, the Nation's capital, the capital of the Free World. The metropolitan Washington area had the highest income and education levels of most major cities in the country. How could it also have so much hate?

She'd come to dread the question and answer session after her speech because they always expected her to have answers that made sense. For a while she'd tried. She'd tried to tell them what the experts told her: that more than a decade of economic retrenchment had put too many people out of work, made them desperate and angry and in need of venting their frustration on some person or group of people they perceived as being to blame. Some social scientists believed that the war in the Persian Gulf had led to increased attacks on both Arabs and Jews — and that quite often, those doing the attacking couldn't tell the difference. But recently, the best she could do was to point the finger at other cities — cities where the problem was so much worse than in Washington.

Tonight that wasn't enough because she knew what they didn't know — about the four dead gay people, one of whom had also been Jewish. She knew that the hate was spreading and she was weak with the knowledge that publicity about the killings could spawn copycat horrors. So, when the final question of the evening came, from an elegant, elderly woman right on the front row, she was not prepared. The woman, swathed in fur and jewels that looked costly even from a distance, was at least seventy and she stood proud and erect, perfectly coiffed silver hair glittering like the diamonds at her ears.

"So, Lieutenant, what can we do?" asked the woman.

"We're here to serve you," Gianna began as usual. "There is a special line into the Hate Crimes Unit that's answered twenty-four hours a day. Any crime that's thought be hate-based . . ."

"No !" The elderly woman pointed a scarlet-tipped finger at Gianna and raised her voice. "I don't care about special lines! I want to know what can we do to stop the hate?"

"I wish I knew," Gianna replied, giving her most truthful answer of the evening.

Mimi surveyed the people who sat with her in a small classroom in the west wing of Metro GALCO for the series of lectures entitled *Out of the Closet and into the World*. There were twenty attendees, a few more men than women, and a representative racial mix, with no more than a ten-year spread, Mimi guessed, in their ages — they all seemed to be between thirty-five and forty-five. She was struck by how ordinary they all looked, by how any of them could be the banker, the government consultant, the association president, or the computer salesman who were dead because, perhaps, they'd once sat in a room just like this one.

Their leader, a professorial looking man of about fifty, sporting a Van Dyke beard and wire rimmed glasses, identified himself as Calvin Cobbs and, sure enough, he was a professor of Sociology at American University. Out of the closet for the last three years, he had made it his mission to assist those willing to make that same transition.

Mimi studied her classmates. Most were merely attentive; several looked nervous; and one woman looked about to pass out from fear. There was, thought Mimi, something vaguely familiar about her.

"So," said Calvin Cobbs, "who would like to tell us what has transpired in your life to bring you to this room?"

The class, in unison, looked around at each other until a trim, handsome young man with fiery red hair and bright blue eyes stood, cleared his throat, and announced: "I'm here because I'm tired of hiding and afraid not to."

They talked and laughed and cried together until the class ended ninety minutes later.

The only sound in the interview room was the almost imperceptible whir of the recording equipment, and the fact that it could be heard was testament to the heaviness of the silence. Eric was aware that he was holding his breath; he didn't want any action of his to be a distraction.

Gianna, anger lurking dangerously close to the surface, leaned her face close in to that of Jack Tolliver, so close that he involuntarily shrank back just the tiniest bit, but it was enough to let Gianna know that his bravado was false, that he would soon answer her questions instead of demanding to know how the police had located him.

"We have our ways, Mr. Tolliver," she'd responded with just enough smugness to make him nervous without telling him that in his case the "way" was nothing short of a miraculous and unexpected blessing: the security camera that Freddy had installed outside his club as much for the protection of the patrons who waited in line for entry as for protection of the property. Tolliver's photo had been on file because he belonged to the Supreme Aryans, a skinhead group under continuing investigation in connection with the vandalism of several synagogues a year ago.

Gianna stepped back to study him. His pale, anemic-looking skin was in sharp contrast to the deep black of his silver-studded leather ensemble: the many-zippered jacket, pants, thick-soled biker boots and cap.

"Why, Mr. Tolliver, were you harassing Freddy Schuyler?"

"I wasn't harassing nobody, I already told ya," he whined.

"The kind of activity you staged outside Mr. Schuyler's place of business on Saturday night could be construed to be a violation of his civil rights, Mr. Tolliver. Not to mention the fact that you were leading an illegal demonstration —"

"I wasn't leading nothing, I tell ya!" he shouted, the fear beginning to show in the tenseness of his body.

"But you were the one doing all the talking. It looked to me like you were the leader, and if you were, then you're in big trouble and I think you should call your attorney. You can use that phone on the table over there."

Gianna deliberately turned her back on the blond with the three earrings, displaying a nonchalance that served its purpose admirably.

"Look, it wasn't my idea," he pleaded. "I was just following orders, doing a job, trying to earn a buck, okay?"

Gianna studied him closely, weighing his response. "I'm supposed to believe that somebody paid you to stand in front of Freddy Schuyler's club and call him a queer? And who printed the flyers — Santa Claus? I don't have time for this crap. Call your lawyer so I don't get in trouble for violating your civil rights. For doing to you what you did to Mr. Schuyler on Saturday night."

"For God's sake, lady, listen to me —"

"Are you gay, Mr. Tolliver?"

Her question caught him off guard and totally flustered him. She now had him where she wanted him and she watched him squirm.

"Well . . . not exactly . . ."

"Is that like being a little bit pregnant?" She laughed and knew that he would think it was directed at him.

"You can't make fun of me!" he protested.

"I wouldn't dream of it. It's just that you confuse me. Either you were in charge on Saturday night or you weren't. Either you're gay or you aren't. I don't do so well with that in the middle stuff."

With a sigh of absolute weariness, Jack Tolliver leaned his head back and closed his eyes. Gianna leaned in close.

"What's the name of your group, Mr. Tolliver?"

"C.Y.K.A.S., but I told you, it's not my group. A lady runs it, a kinda old lady . . ."

Gianna cut him off sharply. "What did you say? Sikes . . . Sacks . . . what?"

"It's letters, C-Y-K-A-S, but I don't know what they mean. The lady, she won't tell nobody. She's really weird, man. Like, I could only call her when she said so, and to a phone booth."

Gianna sagged inside. And because she was frustrated and angry and exhausted from lack of sleep, she put Jack Tolliver through the paces again and again, from the beginning, willing there to be something else, something more, than an old lady and the letters C-Y-K-A-S: letters that meant nothing to Jack Tolliver.

Mimi trotted down Nebraska Avenue behind Calvin Cobbs, an icy fall wind cutting through the insufficient wool of her sweater and slacks. Cobbs moved quickly in his anger and Mimi, trying to talk and run into the wind at the same time, was gasping for breath while still trying to sound both professional and rational. She was granted a reprieve only when Cobbs reached his car and had to fish for his keys deep inside his canvas carryall.

"I'm not planning to sandbag your class," she practically yelled at him. "I told you, I would never do such a thing."

"You're in my seminar under false pretenses. Why should I believe anything you say?" He hissed his anger at her on the wind.

"Listen. If I were planning a blind-side story, do you think I would approach you first, ask for your cooperation? Come on, Mr. Cobbs, you're smarter than that."

He looked at her for the first time, his stare more piercing than the cold. "What do you want, Miss Patterson?"

"I want to know," she said deliberately, "what makes people seek help coming out of the closet. I want to know what happens to them if they decide they can't. I want to know what they're more afraid of: being in the closet or out."

And, she said to herself as she waited for his response, I want to know if you're a killer.

Eric Ashby plopped down in the chair across the desk from Gianna and opened the bag that contained their lunch: Smoked turkey breast sandwiches, salad, milk, and a brownie. They'd promised each other, after they'd both become ill due to lack of sleep and food during their last investigation, that they would always eat a balanced meal at least once a day, regardless of whether they ever got to sleep. He leaned back in the chair, his feet on Gianna's desk, and took a savoring bite of his sandwich. They ate in silence for a while before he began his report.

"For starters, we can place all four victims at Metro GALCO some time in the last year, all in one or the other of the classes on coming out."

"That's good, Eric. What else?"

"Looks like Tolliver's telling the truth, as far as it goes. Nothing incriminating in his apartment. The records from the phone company confirm what he said about the calls he made from his home phone to a pay phone to his contact. The phone is at Union Station so that's a dead end. And to say that our boy is gay is to say that Jack the Ripper was a ladies' man. Tolliver's into heavy S and M. He likes beating people. He's well known in the leather bars and I've talked to several guys who know him, but nobody's ever known him to have a sustained relationship with a man, to care for anyone."

"What about the rest of them, Eric? Something? Anything?"

He shook his head woefully. "Not a peep. Nobody's ever seen or heard of them. They're not associated with any known group or organization. In short, boss, these people are bogus, just like you said they were. How does it feel to be right all the time?"

"If being wrong would find me a killer ..." She trailed off as he shook his head and one-handedly — he was still holding part of a turkey sandwich — rifled through the report.

He held out three pages to her. "You're still batting a thousand. About those parking lots ..."

She sat up straight and gave him a hard look. "You obviously saved the best for last," she said expectantly.

"Joe Murray was in the RFK Stadium parking lot because he was having an affair with Alfie Cane, running back extraordinaire. Phil Tancil was involved with the principal at Washington High. Liz Grayson's car was in the Arena Stage parking lot because she and Susan Jolley had season tickets. And Tony delValle's most recent boyfriend was the teaching pro at the Tennis Center."

Gianna let the words hang there while she considered their meaning; and when clarity came, it brought a new sense of dread. "The killer not only knew those people were gay, he knew who their lovers were," she said in a flat, dead tone.

"That could be a good thing, Anna," Eric said.

But she didn't think so. In fact, something told her that just the opposite was true and once again she found no joy in being right.

"Are these people in the closet, too?"

He shook his head. "Nope. I thought of that, too, but all the lovers are out of the closet. Even Susan

Jolley, who worked for the Army. They all knew she was gay," Eric said, "and the Board of Education knows about the Washington High principal."

She squeezed her eyes shut and pressed her fingers to her temples. Her insides churned and the bile rose in her throat as she accepted the truth that in six days there would most certainly be another dead gay person in another parking lot some place in Washington, D.C. and there seemed little she could do to prevent it.

Mimi hung up the phone, looked at the clock, and sighed. It's payback, she told herself, for all the nights Bev must've watched the clock and waited for me to decide to leave work. Still, she thought, 10:30 on a Friday night is stretching it a bit. Then she laughed at herself. She'd been home all of twenty minutes, time to strip off her clothes, wrap up in a thick robe, and pour a glass of wine. The phone rang and she grabbed it.

"Hi. It's me." Gianna sounded exhausted.

"I just called you. You're not home."

"You're so brilliant," Gianna said teasingly. "I'm in the car, heading uptown ..."

"I'll open the garage door," Mimi said quickly.

"Three minutes," Gianna said.

It was actually four, but Mimi decided to forgive her, seeing the fatigue clouding the clear hazel eyes as Gianna pulled the police-issue white Chevy into the double garage next to the Karmann Ghia. Mimi pushed the button that lowered the door and Gianna stepped out of the car into her arms, her mouth greedy, demanding, her arms drawing Mimi in almost roughly, her hands running up and down Mimi's body. She untied and opened the robe and they both gasped when Gianna's hands made contact with Mimi's nakedness and Mimi went weak in the knees.

"I can't believe I haven't seen you since Sunday."

"Believe it," Mimi gasped as Gianna caressed her nipples. "Take off your clothes," she whispered hoarsely.

Gianna paused long enough to laugh. "You're going to have me on the garage floor?" she asked as her fingers eased between Mimi's legs.

"Stop it!" Mimi shrieked, jumping away from her. "Take off your clothes and put on this robe," she demanded, holding up the mate to the one she wore.

Gianna smiled, shrugged and complied, stripping off her clothes and plunging into the wooly warmth of the robe. Mimi tossed Gianna's clothes inside the kitchen door and walked toward a door in the opposite corner of the garage, beckoning to Gianna who followed gamely.

Mimi opened the door to another world. What was once a tool shed had been converted into a paradise with its centerpiece a six-seater above-ground hot tub, its exterior camouflaged with brick and adobe. Italian tile covered the floor, hothouse plants filled up all four corners of the small room and a domed sky-roof let the moon and stars become part of the landscape. The effect was of a small town Italian piazza. The steam from the tub filled the room, giving a delicious contrast to the chilly garage. Mimi threw her robe onto a low-slung wicker chair.

Gianna laughed out loud. "This is unbelievable! You are just full of surprises!" She threw off her robe and raised her arms to the night sky. Mimi crossed to her and embraced her from behind. Gianna leaned into the embrace with a sigh.

"The first time I saw you you were naked in the steam and I had to pretend I didn't notice."

"You didn't notice!" Mimi insisted. "You just walked away."

"Right into a cold shower." Gianna laughed, turning around to face Mimi. "But that was then and this is now." Gianna kissed her with a gentle urgency that increased in intensity until Mimi was weak-kneed.

Mimi pushed Gianna back into the well-cushioned wicker chair, knelt before her, draped Gianna's legs over her shoulders. She arched upward to meet Mimi's mouth and then, the instant she felt her tongue, she collapsed into the chair, opened her legs totally to the exquisite agony, and released herself to follow the sensation into the night sky. She wanted to ride out there forever but she was riding the wave back, so fast, so fast. She cried out and Mimi held her hands, held on to her.

Mimi rested her face on Gianna's thighs and Gianna toyed with the curly ringlets of Mimi's hair, catching her breath. Then Mimi rose and pulled Gianna to her feet, holding her close for a long moment before releasing her to step into the hot tub. Mimi opened a small refrigerator and removed a bottle of seltzer. Gianna suggested that she bring a bottle of champagne instead.

They luxuriated in the hot, churning water, sipping champagne and learning more about each other, a process prompted by Mimi's demand, "Tell me about you. Where are you from? Why are you a cop? Where's your favorite place in Italy? Why were you celibate for two years?"

Gianna laughed and splashed water on her and told of growing up in a traditional Italian family in Philadelphia, the granddaughter, daughter/ niece, and sister of policemen, and who naturally wanted to be a cop, too, but yielded to family pressure to be the first to attend college since she'd been smart enough to win a partial scholarship to Catholic University.

"So, I came down here to D.C. and after the first semester of classes I applied to take the police department's entrance exam."

"School was that bad?" Mimi asked, laughing.

"It's not that it was bad, I just wasn't interested. I wanted to be a cop, so, when I passed the entrance exam and was admitted to the Academy my sophomore year, I took classes at night and police training during the day."

"You must have been exhausted! When did you sleep?"

"Never! But I'd promised my parents I'd finish college. Then Dad was killed in the line of duty —"

"Gianna! I'm so sorry . . ."

"Yeah. Me, too. It was so stupid. He was trying to prove that all Italians aren't crooks and went solo to bust up some Mafia thing." A frown creased her face as she brought forth the painful memory and she shook her mane of wet hair, like a puppy, to chase it away. "Anyway, with him gone, Mom couldn't afford to help me with tuition which upset her as much as Dad being killed, so I confessed my double life and she cried for about a week before deciding to forgive me and here I am, in a hot tub with you, drinking champagne and thinking impure thoughts about certain parts of your anatomy."

Mimi laughed and reached across the water to pull her close. "You left out some things. Your favorite place in Italy and the small matter of a two-year hiatus . . ."

"You're why the Chief warned me against reporters. You expect all your questions to be answered?"

"Absolutely," Mimi murmured against her hair and Gianna smiled and settled back into her strong arms and talked happily about a tiny village on the Gulf of Gaeta and then less happily about Dorothea who almost two years ago had left to accompany her husband to his new, high-paying job in Arizona.

"She'd long before ceased to love him but, in her words, she'd spent eight years working shitty clerical and secretarial jobs to put him through business school and law school and she was entitled, finally, to the country club life, not to scratching out an existence on a police Lieutenant's salary."

"Police Lieutenants make good money," Mimi said hotly, coming to Gianna's defense.

"Show me where they make two hundred thousand a year and the company car is a Cadillac and I'll take the exam tomorrow. Anyway, for months I was too numb to think about being with anybody. Then I got involved in a couple of back-breaking cases and I didn't have time to think about being with anybody, and by then, it had been so long. . . ." The bubbling hot water churned and the steam rose around them and the flickering candles played shadows against the walls.

"Been down so long seems like up to me," Mimi said musingly.

"You've read that!" Gianna exclaimed, laughing.

"Of course. Hasn't everybody?"

"You're not old enough to have read that."

"How do you know how old I am? I don't know your age."

"Forty. And," Gianna said, moving to the other side of the tub in accurate anticipation of Mimi's reaction, "I'm the police and we can find out all kinds of things."

Mimi shrieked, stood up, hands on hips, attitude at the ready, but momentarily speechless.

"Sit down and come here," Gianna ordered, working hard to suppress laughter as Mimi glared at her indignantly.

"You pulled my file?"

"Of course I did. Now come here, Mimi."

"And you think because you're some hotshot cop you can order me around and expect me to obey?"

"Absolutely. Now come here. Please."

Mimi reluctantly obeyed, sitting on the ledge between Gianna's legs and leaning back into her but still irritated. "You had no right, you know. Background checks are personal and private — a necessary evil — the only way any reporter can obtain police department press credentials. Not even cops can go nosing around in personal background —"

Gianna cut her off with a bite to the back of the neck. "What are you so incensed about? You act like there's some deep, dark secret you don't want discovered. All I saw was brilliance: captain of the debate team, Phi Beta Kappa, enough journalism awards for ten reporters. I saved a lot of time by pulling your file. Now all I need you to tell me is why there was nobody for you after Bev."

But because her hands had begun to move on Mimi's there was little interest in — or need for — the answer to that question.

And they agreed that before one of them drowned it would be a good idea to move to the bedroom, where they remained until late Saturday afternoon when they both went to work.

VIII

"If I tell my wife I'm gay, she'll leave me! She'll take the kids, the house, the car, the dog and the cat! She'll feel hurt and betrayed. How does it help either of us for me to do that? Who benefits?" wailed a man in a blue suit.

The twenty people in the *Hi, Honey, I'm Gay: How to Tell Your Spouse the Truth* seminar looked, almost as a unit, from the man in the blue suit at the back of the room, to Calvin Cobbs at the front, waiting for his response.

"You do," said Cobbs in his gentle, professor's

voice, "because once you're out, you're relieved of the fear that she'll find out. You'll have no more secrets."

"Yeah," offered a glum man in a jogging suit, "and no more job, no more family, no more friends, no more home..."

There was scattered tittering in the room, and even Calvin let a smile lift his lips. Mimi shared an I-know-what-you-mean smile with the glum man who was seated next to her.

Calvin walked down an aisle to stand next to the man in the blue suit, and spoke to him gently, carefully. "How often do you think about telling her?"

"All the time! All the time." The man's misery was palpable.

"And I daresay that holds true for everyone in this room. It's why you're here, isn't it?" Calvin looked around at them as he returned to his perch at the front of the room. "You want to tell them the truth, these people you're married to, because you love them, because you know you're hurting them with your lies about your 'other friends,' about where you are — like tonight. How many of your spouses think you're working late tonight?" He laughed with them as every hand was raised, breaking the tension.

Mimi surveyed the group of ordinary-looking men and women with their not-so-ordinary secret. She thought again of Cedric's words, and then her glance fell on a woman who was seated all the way at the back, in a corner, the quiet, mousy woman from the other seminar, the one had who looked vaguely familiar but whom Mimi couldn't place.

After the class Mimi walked with Cobbs to the parking lot. She'd had to level with him before he'd even give her the time of day, so, swearing him to secrecy she'd shared with him minimal details about the murders and the fact that the only link between the victims was that they'd all attended some kind of class designed to help married gay people come out of the closet.

As they sat in his car, he looked at the photographs she proffered. No, he said, to Elizabeth Grayson and Antonio delValle. But his eyes widened in shock and horror at the photos of Joe Murray and Phil Tancil. Calvin didn't know their names — his was the only name used in class — but he recognized their faces. They'd attended the same lecture series this time last year. And he was certain that the Black guy, Joe Murray, had taken the course twice.

"Do people do that?" Mimi asked with a frown, "come back again?"

"Oh, sure, happens all the time. That scared, funny looking little woman who always sits in the corner? She's been in both classes three or four times. You must understand, Miss Patterson, that some of these people are absolutely terrified. It's not just about angering or disappointing a spouse or losing a house. Some of the women have violent husbands. Some belong to restrictive religions and risk being totally cut off from everything they know . . ."

"Then why do you push them to come out?" Mimi was angry.

"I don't push them to come out, but I do push them to make the process logical and orderly and honest. Remember, Miss Patterson, I've been there. I have three children I'm not allowed to see and my father hasn't spoken to me in four years, but as much pain as I have about that, I can honestly tell you that being relieved of the burden of that secret has changed my life."

Mimi shook her head wearily. "I'm sorry I snapped at you."

"No apologies necessary." He paused and she watched him, watched his face work as he formulated the words to express his thoughts.

"Do you really believe," he asked, "that someone who has attended one of these seminars..." He stopped himself, obviously unwilling to go where the thoughts were taking him. "Is it really possible, Miss Patterson, that a person would use these seminars as a vehicle to do harm?"

"Anything is possible, Dr. Cobbs," Mimi said wearily.

"But do you believe that's what happened?" he pressed.

"I don't know what to believe," she said honestly.

"I hope to God you're wrong," Calvin Cobbs said with prayer in his voice, "and I hope I helped."

He returned the photographs, they shook hands, and she exited his car.

Across the deserted parking lot at her own car, she started the engine, then turned it off. Her imagination was running wild and she couldn't drive under these circumstances. She opened the envelope and removed the photographs of Joe Murray and Phil Tancil. She imagined them sitting in the same room she'd left not thirty minutes earlier, listening to Calvin Cobbs just as she had, perhaps asking the same questions the man in the blue suit had asked tonight: Who benefits? She pictured them telling their wives they had to work late. She pictured them trying to tell their wives the secret of their lives . . .

Holy shit! Another image took over: the tiny group of demonstrators outside Freddy's club, fronted by the loud, rude blond guy but seemingly powered by — the mousy little woman at the back of the class! The one whom Cobbs said had attended three or four times, the one who was also in the other class.

Her mind was in overdrive as she tried to sort out her options. She remembered that Cobbs said no names were used in class, so it would be next week before she'd see the woman again, before she could ask her if she remembered Joe Murray and Phil Tancil and if she knew Tony delValle and Liz Grayson. As she started the car, Mimi felt the buzz inside her that she always got when she knew she'd stumbled onto some important piece of a story. Often she didn't know exactly what the piece was, where it fit, or what it meant. She just knew it existed and that it was important. Whoever that mousy little woman was, she was part of the story.

Gianna, depressed and bone-weary, was stretched out on the couch in her office praying for the relief of sleep that just would not come. Even though she was restless, she was glad she'd requisitioned this particular couch: it was expensive, well-made and a cut above standard government issue furniture. She put in a lot of late nights and thought comfort was worth the price. It was just past six o'clock, and given the pattern to date, the body wouldn't be discovered until after midnight, so she had time for a six-hour nap. More sleep than she'd had in days. If only she could go to sleep.

Images of murderous assault crowded her consciousness no matter how hard she tried to blank the space: the bodies of the dead, their faces, their eyes, the bloody mess that had once been their source of life. And along with those images, the knowledge that not one single shred of evidence existed that could lead her to the killer. These were not crimes that would be solved by evaluating forensic evidence because there was virtually no forensic evidence to be evaluated. Four bullets from the same gun, nothing more — no fingerprints; no hair or fibers; no witnesses, no nothing. Of course, one did consider as evidence the fact that the murderer obviously harbored a deep hatred of homosexuals. Hatred as a clue: A new concept in police investigative techniques, she mused totally without humor. Just be on the lookout for people who hate other people. She fought back the bitter bile that rose inside her. "The only thing that can help me is a mistake. If you make a mistake..." She had spoken out loud and stopped as a knock sounded and the door opened.

The Chief stood framed in the doorway, worry creasing his brow. "I'm sorry, Anna, I didn't mean to wake you..."

"Come on in, Chief. I wasn't asleep." Glad to see him despite her mood, she stood up and yawned as he bounced in on the balls of his feet.

"Judging from that matched set of Samsonite under your eyes, I'd say you haven't slept in days," he said, his rapid-fire delivery softened, she knew, by his concern for her.

"At least," she said, smiling, thankful for a reason to smile.

"By the way, good job on the quarterly crime stats. I like the way you write. Your numbers always help me see the people."

She grimaced and rolled her eyes. He wagged a finger at her. "Don't you do that! Like it or not that kind of stuff comes with the territory, Anna. You're a big gun now, and you're gonna get bigger. If you don't screw it up, that is. I know it's hard to feel like you're on the outside looking in, but it's time you learned to delegate. That's what makes a good leader, and you've got yourself a good follower in Ashby. Use him, and give yourself a rest."

She looked at him in utter amazement, unable to remember the last time she heard so many sentences come from his mouth at the same time. Then, as quickly as he'd come, he was gone and she was staring at a closed door.

For not the first time she wondered at the advisability of having the Chief as her mentor. Not that he'd been the Chief when he took her under his wing. Still . . . She stopped the thought in its tracks. "I may as well get some work done," she said to herself, moving to her desk and switching on the computer, "because I certainly won't get any sleep." But before she could call up her files, there was another knock and this time her boss peered around the corner of the door, gold-rimmed half-glasses perched on his nose.

"Don't get up." He waved her back down and sauntered into the office, parking his butt on the corner of her desk. She couldn't help thinking, as she did almost every time she saw him, that he was one of the most gorgeous men walking. "You know, you wouldn't have to stay here doing this crap at night if you did it during the day when you're supposed to," he said, looking over the glasses at her.

"Yes, sir, Captain Davis. I know," she said calmly.

"Are you being a smartass?" He looked at her closely.

"No, sir, I'm not," she answered truthfully.

"Look here. That was a good quarterly report, Anna. Damn good. And I hear from the B'nai B'rith people that your speech was right on the money. You're good at this Lieutenant stuff, you know, and getting better all the time."

"Yes, sir, I know," she said again.

"But you'd still rather be out there looking for killers."

"Yeah," she sighed, and they were silent for a moment.

"So, what's the deal?" he asked.

"I wish you hadn't asked me that," she said wearily, and when he smiled wryly, she said, "I'm just waiting for the call about the location of the body. I know there will be another one. I know it will be tonight. And I know there's not one damn thing I can do to stop it."

She sank back into her chair, meeting his direct gaze. "And you know what's tearing me up? I've got this feeling there's something available to me that I'm not seeing, or not understanding. And someone will die tonight because I can't figure it out fast enough." Anger and fear and sorrow rose up in her in equal parts.

"One thing you should always remember about being a cop."

"What's that, oh learned one?" Gianna said, letting the bad feelings ebb away for a moment and actually conjuring a smile.

"You're just a cop. That's all. Not a god or a savior or a miracle worker."

He left and she continued to wonder what time the body would be found.

"What the hell do you want?" growled Henry Smith, the night city editor. "I thought I was rid of you when you wrapped that city hall mess." Henry Smith looked like a nineteen-forties movie version of a city editor: he was fat, bald, smoked vile cigars in violation of company policy, cursed incessantly, and had forgotten more about good reporting than any ten of the best reporters could ever hope to know.

"You should be so lucky, Henry. I'm waiting for a body."

"Harbor police just fished one outta the channel. Fucker's prob'ly been dead a week."

"This one would be in a parking lot and newly dead," Mimi said, covering a grin.

"I'll call ya," Henry said, waving her away to spend the empty time wandering around the sparsely inhabited newsroom. She wanted to call Gianna. They'd spent an uncomfortable night together last night, unable to talk, or make love, or sleep, the specter of tonight lurking like a monster in every shadow, Gianna powerless to alter the path of history and in agony because of it, and Mimi equally powerless to soothe her misery. Still she wondered if it wouldn't be a good idea to call ... She wanted to call, to hear the familiar voice, to assure her that no matter what happened in the world ...

She called and there was no answer.

Mimi stared for a moment at the phone in her hand, knowing there could be but one reason for a call to go unanswered in the Hate Crimes office tonight. She looked up at the wall of clocks. In Washington, D.C., it was now 12:20 a.m.

Gianna screeched to a halt beside the gold Mercedes Benz with the prayer that maybe the call was a mistake, that maybe some other cop from some other unit should be here, that maybe this wasn't her case after all.

She and Eric opened their doors simultaneously, he still looking a little peeved that she'd insisted upon driving, as she always did when she was this tense. He strode quickly toward the vehicle as Gianna took note of the remote corner of the underground garage of the high-rent office building and knew her prayer had been in vain. She took in the young security guard who'd probably found the body and then she saw the look on Eric's face.

As she walked around the car toward the driver's side, Eric walked toward her, a hand up as if to stop her from going to the car, but he lowered it when they reached each other. "Anna ... this one's ... I don't know ..."

She brushed past him to the car and looked in and pain tore across her heart, an agony so sharp and sudden that it closed her eyes and she almost made the unforgivable error of reaching out to the car to support herself. She opened her eyes and looked into the dead ones of a woman who could have been Mimi; a young, lovely, rosewood-colored woman with a head full of untamed curly ringlets. She could have been Mimi had her face not been contorted with the agony of death, had her eyes not been drained of love and hope and joy. Gianna wanted to break down and cry but instead she surveyed the interior of the fifty-thousand-dollar death chamber: the honey-colored leather seats now stained dark by the woman's blood; the computerized console seeming to belong in an aircraft instead of an automobile; the telephone that had not helped save her life. This woman had been murdered like the others, genitalia obliterated by a powerful weapon at close range. The difference here, Gianna saw, was that this victim had fought, had struggled against death. She had not gone gently into that place, but with anger and defiance. This victim, in her agony, had ripped the leather seats, tearing out several fingernails in the process; had tried in vain to reach the telephone, which was on the floor; had tried to open the door she hadn't realized was locked. Gianna studied the trails of blood left by the maimed fingers . . .

She forced herself away from the horror and turned to Eric, who had followed her, his red hair in flaming contrast to his white, bloodless face.

"It took her a long, awful time to die." Eric choked on the words and Gianna put a hand on his arm to steady him, to steady herself, for the long night ahead. She closed her eyes briefly and saw the dead woman's face again — a face at least ten years younger than those of the other four victims.

"She's younger than the others. Can that mean anything?"

"My guess would be no," Eric said.

Gianna agreed. She'd been grasping at straws again — looking for something, anything, to hold onto.

The image coursed through her like an electric charge and she whirled around and sprinted the few steps back to the Mercedes and leaned inside. This time the smells assaulted her: the rich, new-leather odor mingled with the dead woman's perfume, both of them overpowered by the harsh, metallic smell of blood and the indescribable smell of death. Gianna caught her breath as she found what she sought: There were no keys in the ignition. In all the other cases the keys had been in the ignition. No keys here in the big Benz, and the doors had been locked. A break. The first real break in this case. Gianna wanted to shout.

"Seal this building, Eric. Nobody in, nobody out. Station somebody at every elevator, at every stairway, on the roof, in the boiler room, in the lobby. And when we find out who she was, where she worked, seal that floor and the ones above and below."

Eric moved swiftly to obey and she turned to find the uniformed security guard who looked about ready to expire from fear. Gianna didn't blame him. He was in for a tough time.

It took her fifteen minutes to get him to admit that he'd not made the first security sweep at eleven o'clock as required because he'd been playing one of those new computerized sports games with the guard in the lobby. But after she assured him that being fired was the least of his worries his information proved helpful: the woman in the car was Carolyn somebody, a lawyer with a big firm that occupied the entire eighth, ninth and tenth floors, and she very often worked late. She did not, however, usually park her car on this level which was why the guard came over to take a look.

"You wouldn't have looked anyway?" Gianna asked.

"No," he said, with a shrug, a gesture that brought all Gianna's rage to the surface.

"Why the hell not?" she yelled at him.

"Patterson!"

Sardonic Henry Smith bristled with urgency and when Mimi trotted over to him, he was glowering in self-righteous indignation at the police scanner. "Some kind of bloody double talk all over the goddamn radio! Can't understand a fuckin' thing they're saying! Is this the CIA or what? Listen to this shit, will ya? Not a word of it makes a damn bit of sense!"

Mimi could only take Henry's word for it, since she was never adept at deciphering police radio jargon. "What are they saying, Henry?"

"Haven't you been listening to me, Patterson? I

don't know what the fuck they're saying! It's all coded and scrambled. The only thing I've been able to pick up is that it's downtown somewhere and maybe in an underground car park. Patterson, what are you up to now?"

Mimi felt cold inside, and more than a little scared. "Henry, I need some help on this one."

"Do I get a story out of it?"

"Nope. Sorry."

"The hell you are. Take Phillips. He's not doing anything."

The cub reporter, a pale, scraggly boy in his early twenties followed Mimi out of the building and into the parking lot, breathing hard with the effort to keep up.

Mimi told him to cruise the downtown business district between 16th and 22nd Streets and between K and P Streets and said a silent prayer of thanks that this was tiny little Washington, D.C. and not New York or L.A. or Chicago where downtown meant a universe.

"Unless of course you see an emergency response vehicle."

"Ah, what's that?" Phillips asked.

"An ambulance, police car, or fire truck," Mimi snapped, thinking that this boy was as dumb as he looked.

"Oh, yeah, right. And whaddya want me to do if we see one?" he asked with a nonchalance that made Mimi physically ill. If she'd been this inept as a cub reporter, she'd have been fired.

"I want you to follow it," Mimi said between

130

clenched teeth, literally biting back the response she wished she could give Phillips.

They were cruising in the service lane on K Street just east of 20th Street when an unmarked detectives' sedan whizzed by them, lights flashing but no siren, and turned right on 20th.

"Follow!" yelled Mimi.

"What?" the hapless Phillips queried.

"That black car, goddammit, are you crazy or what?"

Mimi slammed her hand into the dash, scaring Phillips into action. He crashed his foot into the gas pedal and the rattletrap news car jumped forward like its rabbit namesake. When they turned the corner Mimi saw the flashing lights and the knot of official cars in front of a brand new twelve-story office building on the north side of the street. She whipped her press credentials out of her purse and put them around her neck, in plain and easy view for the cops, and suggested that Phillips follow suit. When he mumbled that he'd forgotten to bring his, Mimi opened the door and got out of the car even though it was still moving.

She trotted up to the entrance of the building's underground parking garage, nodded at the cops positioned there, and followed the activity down to the third level where her eyes immediately focused on Gianna standing adjacent to a gold-colored car, whose make and model she couldn't discern through the swarm of police personnel surrounding it. When Mimi looked again at Gianna, what she saw startled her: a cold rage that she would have denied Gianna capable of possessing, and it was directed at a cowering security guard who was desperately trying to explain something.

"Why the hell not?" she heard Gianna yell and the guard shook his head in abject misery.

Mimi tried to work her way toward the rear of the car to get a glimpse of the license plate.

Gianna saw her. Their eyes met and held for an instant before Gianna turned and said something to a plainclothes detective who bore down on Mimi with such speed and purpose that she didn't have time to back up before he was upon her.

"You'll have to clear this area immediately, Miss."

"I'm Montgomery Patterson from the —"

"I don't care if you're the Baby Jesus. You gotta clear this area right now. Come with me please."

Since it was not a request Mimi preceded him up the ramp and out of the garage but she balked at being hustled across the street to stand behind the yellow tape.

"You can't make me stand over here!" she protested.

"Wanna bet," he drawled, totally non-threateningly, and he left her there behind the tape and returned to the garage.

Mimi waited until he was out of sight and then circled the gathering crowd toward the front door of the building. Three uniforms in the lobby. Cursing, she darted along the side of the building into the alley and toward the rear entrance, knowing it was a waste of time but having to do it anyway. Gianna had been thorough. Three uniforms there, one of whom demanded to see her credentials and shone his light in her eyes when he compared the ID photos with her face. She was stopped and credentialed twice more in the alley behind the building before she decided to give up.

The night was cold, she was hungry, and she certainly wasn't worried about any details leaking to other news agencies. Gianna had completely closed off access to the building — and to the story. Gianna had also closed access to herself, but that was a thought Mimi didn't want to have at that moment.

Back on 20th Street, she looked for Phillips, hoping he'd been snooping around, had seen or heard something useful. She found the car, Phillips inside, eyes closed, mouth open, snoring. She kicked the side of the car scaring him green and stalked off in the direction of M Street and Georgetown, and her best hope for a taxi in the somnolent capital of the Free World at 1:30 a.m.

Mimi awoke suddenly to a sound, familiar but unexpected. She sat up in bed to attune herself to whatever had awakened her. The red-eyed digital clock glowed 5:15 a.m. The garage door? Yes, now it was descending with its customary thud. She jumped up, threw on her robe and stumbled into the kitchen just as Gianna opened the door. Mimi, appalled at the sight of her, led her to the bedroom and helped her undress.

"I need a shower. I have exactly three hours to sleep then I have to go back. She looked like you, Mimi. She was beautiful, smart, successful. A lawyer, high-powered, lots of money. She was thirty-three years old and she has a two-year-old child."

Gianna crumpled and Mimi caught her, held her, held onto her, until the shakes stopped. Then she got into the shower with her, washed her, put her to bed, and watched her sleep.

And while Gianna slept, fitfully, her brow creased with the images, details of her work that wouldn't recede even in sleep, Mimi tried to imagine how it would feel to look down at death and see a loved one.

Then she laughed at her ego. Who says she loves you, Mimi Patterson? She's never said that. "But I love you," Mimi whispered and smoothed the crease in her brow. "I love you," she whispered again, even though her mind was already formulating the story she knew she had to write, the story that would most likely drive a wedge between her and this woman she loved.

"I will not mention the cause of death, Tyler, period, end of discussion." And to amplify her point, Mimi switched off the computer and stood up.

"Where are you going?" Tyler demanded.

"Police headquarters. Nobody who knows anything will talk to me on the phone." She winced at how great an understatement that was. Nobody who knew anything would even answer the phone.

"Patterson, the cause of death is crucial to this story."

"It absolutely is not." Mimi added even more adamantly, "What's crucial to this story is the fact that a bloody maniac is murdering gay people who thought they were safely in the closet."

"We have a responsibility to the readers..." Tyler began.

Mimi cut him off with a razor sharp retort. "We have a responsibility to Hispanic gay women —"

It was his turn to cut her off. "What the hell are you talking about?"

"Try to pay attention, Tyler." She enumerated on her fingers as she spoke. "White male, Black male, Hispanic male. White female, Black female. Even you can figure out who's next, Tyler. About this same time next month. Just in time for Christmas. *Feliz Navidad.*"

He opened and closed his mouth a couple of times then shook his head and stalked off.

Gianna sat looking at the photographs from Carolyn Green's car and had to close her eyes to the horror of it. She'd never before had this reaction to a crime scene. Maybe it was because the woman reminded her of Mimi.... She looked again at the destruction inside the Mercedes Benz, the proof that Carolyn Green, unlike the other victims, was conscious and alive long enough to put up a struggle. Gianna pushed the photos across the desk, away from her and asked again the questions that plagued her:

"How did the phone get on the floor, Eric? If she'd gotten her hands on that phone she wouldn't have dropped it, I'm certain. And where the hell are the car keys? Why was the driver's side door locked and the passenger side door unlocked? I think our killer has finally made a mistake and we damn well better take full advantage of it."

She was up and pacing, wound so tightly she appeared ready to rupture.

"In all five deaths, the killer is sitting right there in the car. Do they argue first? Is there a visible threat from the killer? That can't be the case because the victim wouldn't just sit there. So, the victim doesn't expect the gun and when the shot comes they're so surprised they just give up and die. But this time was different. This time the victim got mad instead of scared. This time the victim fought back. Maybe she grabbed him, struck out at him, scratched him . . ."

Gianna drew the awful images toward her again as if they were some kind of oracle, as if they held some message, some clue, a solution.

This was the fifth set of such photos, so familiar yet so very different. Carolyn Green had been determined not to die. That, or . . .

"You're making me nervous pacing around like that. You never pace. What's on your mind?" Eric asked.

"The psychological profiles I've been reading indicate a specific trait or pattern of behavior with certain serial killers. In these murders, it's the extreme neatness of the vehicles. Until now. This car is a mess, and I don't think Carolyn Green did it all. I think our pal snapped. Something's thrown him over the edge and I'll bet he left lots of goodies for us to find — skin and blood and hair and maybe even a few good prints." She made a sound in her throat and moved abruptly to the door.

He looked at her with concern. "Where are you going?"

"To look at the enlargements."

He half stood and she waved him back down. "You don't need to go. I confess I'm obsessed and about to lose my mind. No need for you to share. Lean on the lab. Don't let Asa Shehee out of your sight."

She opened the door to find Mimi standing there, hand raised preparing to knock. They stood looking at each other.

"What the hell are you doing here?" Eric thundered, looking at Mimi with a shocked amazement that mirrored her own at seeing him in Gianna's office. He crossed quickly to the door and inserted himself between them.

He glowered at Mimi and said to Gianna, "She's from the seminar at Metro GALCO, the one on how to tell your spouse you're gay." He turned to Mimi. "What are you doing here?"

Mimi said with more calm than she felt, "I'm sorry to shock you. I'm Montgomery Patterson from the . . ."

He cut her off with a snort of disgust. "The reporter! You've got a lotta nerve! In that seminar under false pretenses."

She tried out a half grin on him. "And how many of us knew you were a cop?"

"I've got a job to do, lady!" he bellowed at her.

Mimi looked from Eric to Gianna, all traces of the smile gone. "So do I. Lieutenant, I'd appreciate a few moments of your time —"

Eric interrupted. "I don't know what kind of game you're playing, but you can't play it here."

"Eric," Gianna said calmly, having managed to shift feelings and emotions into a professional gear, "if you would excuse us for just a moment."

"But Anna — Lieutenant, I don't think —"

"I'd appreciate it if you'd prepare the enlargements. I'll be there in just a few moments."

Eric turned abruptly and stalked off down the hall.

Gianna gently closed the door and stood looking at Mimi. "I gather you're doing a bit of undercover work," Gianna said quietly, studying Mimi.

"It was the only thing that made sense. Your . . . colleague sits next to me. He always seemed like such a nice guy."

"Detective Ashby is a very nice guy," Gianna said with a hint of defensiveness, "and a damn good cop."

"We don't use our names in the seminar," Mimi said, hoping to somehow ease the tension that was building between them.

"Why didn't you tell me about it?"

"Because we . . . I thought we kind of agreed not to discuss our work on this case," Mimi said.

Gianna closed her eyes briefly and walked to the window. She looked down on the scurrying shapes in the square below, all bundled up against the cold, and shivered. "I take it you're here in an official capacity now," she said, turning to face Mimi.

"Yes. I'd like to know the name of the woman who was murdered last night, to know something of her background."

"But I told you about her . . ." Gianna stopped herself.

"You didn't tell Montgomery Patterson, Lieutenant," Mimi said.

"May I ask," Gianna said carefully, "why you don't know? You knew about the others."

"Because," Mimi said with a small smile, "you've shut out my source at the FBI."

Gianna's eyes widened in understanding. "Don somebody?" Mimi nodded and Gianna asked, "What's his interest? Why is he nosing around this case?"

"He's my editor's boyfriend. Two of the victims were their friends. His interest is totally unofficial and personal, but it's how I ended up on this story."

"I couldn't figure why the Bureau was interested since we hadn't asked for help." Gianna almost smiled but her fatigue was too great. She picked up the file on Carolyn Green, removed a couple of pages, and gave them to Mimi who read quickly and wrote in her notebook before returning the pages to Gianna with thanks.

"You need to know," Mimi said quietly, "that I'm doing a story for Sunday's paper —"

Gianna cut her off with a gasp. "Mimi, you can't!"

"I have to, Gianna. This thing is way out of control —"

"I don't need you to tell me that! I need you to understand what could happen if you panic the public, or, worse, send the murderer into hiding."

"Gianna, I can't sit on this story any longer. I have an obligation to the public just as you do."

"Or to your publisher to sell papers?"

Gianna's bitter, cutting tone startled Mimi. "That's not fair and you know it."

"Mimi, I'm asking you, please, don't do this story. It not only could but probably would jeopardize our investigation."

"That means you know more than you did last week."

Gianna shook her head. "I can't answer that."

Mimi crossed to the door. "I'm sorry, Gianna," she said softly and left without looking back, knowing that if she did, what she saw would take precedence over any story and over anything else in the world.

Gianna watched her depart with a mixture of sensations welling inside her: a crucial emptiness but also a full measure of pain and fear and desire. For the first time in eighteen years — since she joined the Department — she wished she had another job, the kind that didn't ask her to make choices, the kind that didn't get in the way of her life.

She looked at the photograph of her father, the one she'd put in the Art Deco frame to jazz up the solemn young cop in the old-time uniform. The father she'd adored but whom she'd rarely seen because he was too busy being a cop. It had been his life. All he ever wanted, all he ever cared about. She'd patterned herself after him in admiration of his dedication, even though that dedication had cost him the love of his wife, cost him the daily interaction with his children, cost him his life.

"There's only one way to be a cop," she remembered him telling her mother after one of their many arguments over his never being at home, "and that's all the way!" *I'm an all the way cop, too,* Gianna thought, and as she heard the words reverberate inside her she flung open the door and hurried out of the office and down the hall to the Think Tank.

She entered and was enveloped by the photographic enlargements of the five crime scenes. Her eyes instinctively, immediately went past Eric to the photo of Carolyn Green, her lifeless eyes wide open in the shocked surprise of anticipating her death.

"Look at her! She's more surprised than anything else. Not the shock or fear of the others but surprise," Gianna said to Eric, thinking that she would have liked Carolyn Green had she known her.

"But wouldn't they all be surprised?"

And Gianna was the one surprised to hear the Chief's voice because until he spoke she hadn't realized he was present.

"Yes. But this is different. I'll explain later. I'm glad you're here because finding you was my next stop. You should know that Mimi Patterson's doing a story for Sunday's paper —"

"Damn!" Eric exploded and threw a sheaf of papers into the air, giving Gianna a moment to recover from the stinging hurt of saying Mimi's name out loud.

The Chief was watching her closely. "How much does she know?" he asked calmly.

"Enough," Gianna said with a shrug.

"I assume all your charm and other efforts to change her mind failed," he said dryly, still watching her.

Gianna turned away from him and pretended to study the blown-up death scenes, willing her voice to be steady, normal, and wondering whether she'd misread or misunderstood the innuendo his question contained. "You assume correctly. She said things were too far out of hand to sit on the story any longer."

Eric snorted and the Chief chuckled. "That sounds like her. But believe me, Anna, it could be worse. It could be one of those TV types going off half cocked and scaring the shit out of people. Mimi is a good reporter, and a fair one. She won't hurt you."

"Does that mean you want me to cooperate with the press?" Gianna asked through a sinking feeling. Loving Mimi had done nothing to temper her general dislike of the city's news media.

"Now you're getting the hang of it," the Chief said with a wry grin. "Damn right I'd rather have direct quotes from you and me in the newspaper than a bunch of no-comments to fuel speculation that we haven't got the first clue. Come on, let's you and me go find your friend, Captain Davis, and then go huddle with the public affairs people and cook up some statements that sound like we're in control of this thing." He charged out of the room.

Gianna exchanged a look with Eric and followed the Chief to the third floor public affairs office.

IX

They could have saved their time, plans and schemes.

True to her promise, Mimi reported only those facts that she had learned independent of Gianna — which meant that she did not include the cause of death. She merely reported that the circumstances of the murders were "grisly." The story, which spread across three columns on the front page and filled an entire page inside the paper, was, Gianna grudgingly admitted, accurate and fair and balanced and generously sprinkled with quotes from the Chief of

Police and the head of the Hate Crimes Unit, who said she was confident the case would be resolved within the week.

But it wasn't Mimi's story that created the firestorm of reaction so intense that even the Chief was taken by surprise. It was the follow-up stories done by the tabloids and the TV news outlets that made the murders the hottest topic in Washington since the Capitol Hill sex scandals. One paper carried the headline, *Son of Sam Stalks Gay Washington!* And one of the TV stations dubbed the crimes "The Front Seat Murders." Criticism from every segment of the public flew at the police department in general, and at the Hate Crimes Unit in particular.

The entire metropolitan area, it seemed, was consumed with speculating on the meaning of "grisly," and some of the more inventive rumors rivaled the truth for awful. Some family members of the victims were outraged that the secret their loved ones had carried with them to their graves was now a matter for public discussion; and the bank where Phil Tancil had been a vice president issued a statement insisting it had been unaware of Tancil's "sexual proclivities." The mayor, already irritated that her city was known as the Murder Capital of America, was furious that once again the place was painted as sinister and dangerous. And some City Council members were making noises about wasting money on the Hate Crimes Unit.

So fierce was the reaction from all quarters that Gianna was ordered to hold a press conference Tuesday afternoon to reassure the public, especially the terrified and outraged gay and lesbian

144

community, that law and order still prevailed, that they would not be systematically eliminated, one by one, while they sat inside their automobiles.

Later, Gianna and her team sat around the table in the Think Tank and watched the television news programs: watched Tony delValle's wife collapse in tears as she was cornered by a TV news camera crew on her front porch as the reporter yelled questions at her; watched — and cheered — as Carolyn Green's husband outran and slammed the door in the face of another camera crew attempting a similar ambush; listened to her own words misinterpreted and misconstrued by the serious-faced six o'clock news reader. But what moved Gianna was the fear she saw in the faces of the gays and lesbians on the TV screen, and she wondered, as the news reader suggested, if she, Lieutenant Maglione, really was responsible for that fear.

She was jolted out of her reverie by an angry Cassandra Ali yelling at the television screen.

"You lying son of a bitch! Where do they get this shit? Can we sue them or something? Did you hear what he said, Anna? I mean Lieutenant." The rookie quickly gained control of herself.

"Actually, Cassie, I didn't . . ."

"He said you were gonna be replaced as chief of this unit or maybe even the unit would be disbanded! Can't we make them retract that or something?" Gianna worked to cover a smile at the young woman's righteous fury. Oh to be that young again.

"I don't know, Cassie. That's why we have Legal Affairs and Public Affairs. They get paid to worry about stuff like that. We, on the other hand, get paid to catch murderers." And cocking her head toward the TV, she thought: Which we obviously don't do very well.

She stood, stretched, checked her watch. Just five-thirty, but the winter darkness made it feel much later. So, too, no doubt, did the recent lack of sleep.

"Where are you off to?" Eric asked warily when she took her coat and purse off the rack.

"I'll be back in about an hour," she said carefully. And, pointing to the TV, added, "You all shouldn't watch any more of that crap. It's not good for your digestion."

Mimi got up to answer the doorbell, fully prepared to maim or kill whoever was dumb enough to be at her door this night. Her surprise at finding Gianna was tinged with an inexplicable foreboding, and when Gianna evaded her embrace, her feeling was confirmed. A chill invaded her body as she followed Gianna into the den.

"Why didn't you use the garage door opener?" Mimi asked.

"I'm not staying. I need to get back. . . ."

Gianna's response was distracted, tentative. She'd turned away from Mimi to stand before the wall of bookshelves and was absently fingering the book spines when Mimi moved to stand close behind her.

"What is it, Gianna?"

Gianna turned to face her, her eyes clouded with fatigue and hurt and something Mimi couldn't name.

"I can't . . . handle it, Mimi."

"You can't handle what, Gianna?" Mimi was frozen inside.

"You. This case. Together. I can't . . ."

"Gianna, please don't do this."

"I understand you have a job to do but I can't handle what I feel when your job interferes with mine, and I can't allow you — I can't allow anyone to get in the way of my job. People's lives depend on how well I do —"

"You think I don't know that?" Mimi grabbed Gianna's arm and pulled her close. "Do you think I would do anything, that I would ask you to do anything, that would jeopardize people's lives?"

"You did that story, Mimi." Gianna pulled away angrily. "You jeopardized my investigation, and I asked you not to do that."

"I have a responsibility too, Gianna, and it's not to the police department." Mimi was stung by the accusatory tone of Gianna's voice. "The public has a right to know there's a serial killer out there, especially that segment of the population that's vulnerable."

"The public has a right to expect protection and I can't give it if I have to worry that my lover will undermine my efforts."

Mimi was stunned into momentary silence. She searched Gianna's face looking for proof that she really didn't believe what she'd just said.

"Where do you think the line is, Gianna, between the police department's need to protect its investigation and the public's need for information to protect itself?" Mimi asked carefully.

"I didn't come here to argue semantics with you. I don't have time for that." Gianna's anger had not diminished.

"It's not semantics, it's a real issue. It's a real problem that the press and the police need to fix and I'd like to think that you and I can —"

Gianna cut her off with icy anger. "I asked you not to run a story."

"I don't work that way. I never have and I never will." Now Mimi was angry.

They stood facing each other, holding each other with their eyes for a long moment before Gianna spoke — softly but with traces of anger still lingering.

"If whatever we have between us is to survive this case —"

Mimi cut her off with razor-sharp swiftness. "Don't call it 'whatever,' Gianna. It has a name, what we have between us. Don't you know what it is? Or are you afraid to call it by that name?" Mimi was both hurt and angry.

Gianna looked into her eyes, into her heart, into her soul, probing and seeking and Mimi thought for an instant that some tiny thing flickered in the hazel depths but then it was gone.

Gianna said, "I'm going now, Mimi."

"Please don't do this, Gianna. Please don't."

"I don't know what else to do, Mimi," said the all the way cop as she opened the door and quickly left without turning around so that Mimi would not see the tears that filled her eyes and overflowed and ran in tiny streams down her face as she ran the last few steps to her car.

148

And as she sped downtown, numbed by the ache inside, almost blinded by the tears, she answered the question posed to her scant moments earlier: Yes, I know what lives between us and yes, I am afraid.

She activated lights and siren to clear the southbound 16th Street traffic that was in her way and she rolled down the windows and let the icy wind dry her tears so that when she pulled into the police garage her eyes only looked tired and red as usual from lack of sleep.

She unlocked the door to the Think Tank and turned on the lights. The enlargements still hung on the walls and reports were stacked neatly on the table for her inspection. Eric had left a note explaining that he'd sent everybody home to bed and he was with Carolyn Green's husband. He just realized, after seeing the news report, that the man was a college friend because Carolyn Green used her own name and not her husband's. He'd meet her back here at 10:00 pm sharp and maybe they could have a drink before calling it quits for the night. And he'd added two postscripts: Did she think it important that Carolyn Green planned to leave her husband for her woman lover? Call Asa Shehee ASAP.

"Hi, Doc, I'm returning your call," Gianna replied to the forensics man's growled "Whatdoyouwant?" phone greeting.

His tone changed dramatically when he heard who it was. "Listen, kiddo, I just want you to know you did the right thing not going public with these crimes."

"If this is what right feels like —"

He cut her off with his grizzly-bear growl. "Dammit, woman, this is the kind of killer who'd go underground at the mere whiff of notoriety, not the egomaniac who thrives on it. And if you're not close to a bust, my guess is you'll never get her — and copycat killers will crawl out of the woodwork to make things even worse."

"What did you say?" Gianna literally couldn't believe her ears. *"Her?"* Was Shehee saying the killer was a woman?

"Preliminary test results on blood, tissue, fiber samples from the Mercedes — you called it right when you figured the Green victim tangled with the killer."

Gianna hung up and looked up at the photo of the dead woman, at the images of her horrible death, and silently thanked her for her courage. "I'll try not to let you down," she said, and turned with renewed vigor to the stack of files and reports before her.

From Cassandra Ali, a note attached to a lengthy research document regretted no record of homicides on the 21st of the month existed that could tie into these gay-related killings. Kenny Chang's report said no serial killer had been released from jail or any other institution within the continental United States or Canada in the last five years. Linda Lopez's report listed the names of a dozen recent parolees known to have killed from a specifically sexual motivation, and noted that while investigation was ongoing, a preliminary check showed that none had ties to the Washington area. Someone had affixed a note to the outside of Phil Tancil's file — a note from the security guard who'd found the body, asking the police to please alter the entry in his official log book to show that Tancil was found on the 22nd and not the 21st.

Gianna frowned, opened the file, and removed the guard's log book. She paged through it, impressed again with his detailed neatness. She turned to the last page for which there was an entry and examined his carefully printed notation: *Mon. Oct. 21, 91, 12:30am.*

Gianna scrutinized those cryptic symbols, amazed at the fact of their simple truth: When Ed Coleman had clocked in for his shift it was, indeed, Monday, the 21st of October. But when he found Phil Tancil's body, it was, in fact, Tuesday, the 22nd. The same was true for all five victims. Even if the official time of death was early evening of the 21st — as was true for Tony delValle and Phil Tancil — all official reports and documents were dated the 22nd or later.

Her fingers fumbled at the computer keys, entering the wrong codes twice before she accessed the National Computer Information Center, and she cursed out loud at the program's time and information limitations. She then called up the Nexus program that would print out any newspaper story on any murder in the tri-state area on any 22nd day of the month, and for a week thereafter, for any year. Finally, a twenty-year old front page story in the four Washington papers of that time. Two were dated October 25, 1971, the others a day later, and all were about the murder of the Reverend Alexander Brathwaite. "This is it," she said aloud when she read the headline of the first article: Prominent Minister Slain in Church Parking Lot.

The Reverend Alexander Brathwaite, pastor of a

prosperous Presbyterian congregation in the prosperous D.C. suburb of Montgomery County, Maryland, had joined a metropolitan ecumenical group and agreed to volunteer one day a week in an inner-city Washington prison ministry. It was 1970 and the fervor of the Civil Rights Movement still burned brightly. The young Rev. Brathwaite believed passionately in the teachings of another young minister who had been murdered just two years earlier for the passion of his beliefs. In fact, said his friends, Alex Brathwaite fancied himself a white Martin Luther King, and was proud of the rapport he had so easily developed with the largely non-white prisoners he believed himself destined to save.

The excitement of Washington and an activist ministry soon left Alex Brathwaite bored with his tame-by-comparison suburban church, so when several of the other activist young ministers hit upon the notion of establishing a non-denominational congregation open to all regardless of race, gender, or sexual preference, Brathwaite leaped at the chance to become part of this mission.

Gianna jumped when she read the name of her friend, Art Crawford, as one of the young ministers involved in that radical-for-its-time project. She resisted the urge to call him and forced herself to continue to read how Brathwaite accepted the job as head of the inner-city ministry, spending almost all his time in Washington and leaving his wife, Jessica, and their two young children at home in the suburbs while he immersed himself in a new world: a world of Spanish-speaking people, of Black people, of socially and politically and culturally and economically different people, people with whom his young wife was unfamiliar and uncomfortable; people who did not interest or amuse or challenge her as they did her husband. The article quoted the wife as calling the people of her husband's ministry "Godless and godforsaken sinners."

Gianna rubbed her eyes and tried to knead some of the tension from her neck. She could feel where the story would lead. She forced herself to take the time to read the lengthy article in its entirety instead of skipping to the end.

Jessica Brathwaite, angered at her husband's lengthy absences from home, would suddenly and irately appear at either the Ministry headquarters in a dilapidated section of Southwest Washington, or at one of the Ministry's three community centers in an equally dingy part of Northwest D.C., looking for Alex, demanding that he come home to her and their children. A stoic Rev. Brathwaite would apologize to those present and leave with his wife, only to reappear the next day with the pronouncement that "Jessie would soon get the hang of a community ministry." But Jessie never did and on the evening of July 21st, 1971, she came looking for Alex again. This time she brought a gun with her. She found him, along with an associate named Herb Addison, in his car in the parking lot of the Church Street Center and, according to the peculiar brand of gentility dictated by times, "... she shot Rev. Brathwaite in a brutal manner and arranged his body in a prayerful pose."

"... in a prayerful pose." The words reverberated in her head. The date, the car, the brutal manner of the murder, the prayerful pose. Here, surely, was the killer, and yet ...

The police found Jessica at her suburban Maryland home early the next morning, sitting in a rocking chair and reading the Bible to her children, her clothes still splattered with her husband's blood. Jessica Brathwaite was found not guilty of murder by reason of insanity and confined to the ward for the criminally insane at St. Elizabeth's Hospital, the same ward, Gianna thought numbly, that had been home over the years to such diverse psychopaths as Ezra Pound and John Hinckley.

Snatching up the phone, she hurriedly dialed the Records Section and ordered the Alex Brathwaite murder file; then, just as quickly, she rang Art Crawford, pastor of Metropolitan Community Church, Washington's non-denominational gay church, who was, she knew, a dedicated workaholic. He answered his office phone on the second ring. He was surprised and delighted to hear from her.

"Alex Brathwaite?" he yelped when Gianna told him what she wanted. "Of course I remember him, he was one of my closest friends. We were at seminary together. What could you possibly want to know about Alex?"

"Everything, Art. Everything you know, everything you can remember."

She heard him sigh. She was asking for a lot: for twenty-year old memories that had certainly dimmed with time; for information that could be intensely personal about someone who was once a friend: for a minister to reveal what would in her line of work be considered privileged information.

She waited respectfully in the silence that

allowed the Rev. Arthur Crawford to make up his mind about what — if anything — he would reveal. Finally she heard him clear his throat and he began to talk about Alex, the son of fundamentalist missionaries whose zeal to save the souls of the unenlightened had led them all over the world, their only child in tow. And of course that child could only follow in their zealous footsteps.

"The poor guy didn't have a chance," Art said sadly. "He could not have been anything other than a minister. That he found the nerve to stand up to them and refuse to be a missionary I know was the hardest thing he ever did in his life."

"He didn't want to be a minister?" Gianna asked.

"He didn't know what he wanted, Gianna. I'm telling you the guy never had a chance to think about it. His parents rammed it down his throat and that's wrong, no matter how right the reason. I'd guess that being a preacher is a lot like being a cop: You either get the calling or you don't, and if you try to do the job without the calling, you'll be miserable."

An all the way cop, an all the way preacher. Gianna felt every bit of the passion of Art's words and she had to force her mind and her emotions to stay with the issue at hand. "The old newspaper article I just read made him sound like a good minister," she offered.

"He was wonderful," Art said simply. "Compassionate, generous, dedicated, tireless — all the right things. But he was innately all those things anyway. That's the kind of human being he was. You know, I always thought he took on the Community Ministry job just to spite his parents."

155

"How? I would think they'd have loved the idea. Kind of like doing their missionary work but in an urban setting," Gianna said.

"Alex saw it exactly the opposite. I remember he made them furious as they were about to leave on a trip to some African country. He explained that centuries before the Europeans, the Africans had language and art and culture and a civilization and religion, but it was due solely to the interference of whites that they'd lost those things. 'The only thing you can possibly save them from,' Alex had told them, 'is yourselves.' " Art chuckled softly to himself at the memory and then was silent. Gianna allowed it for as long as she could, then asked the question that had lurked between the lines of the twenty-year old newspaper story.

"When did he know he was gay, Art? Was that something you shared with him?"

"Lord no!" Art exclaimed with a bark of laughter. "Not only didn't we share it, we didn't even talk about it. I honestly don't think Alex had a clue about his homosexuality until we began the community ministry and he encountered homosexuals for the first time. I can still see the look on his face when I told him I was gay. At first he truly didn't understand. But then, when he did, he was the most kind and gentle and loving and supporting of all the ministers. The rest of them wanted to toss me out the door, good Christians that they were. Alex was the one who stood up for me, who reminded our brethren of our mission. It was Alex, true missionary that he was, who always was able to love every person no matter what. It was Alex who was good. Always good."

Gianna conjured up another image from the ancient newspaper story, that of a young wife left home alone in a strange city with two young children and thought: No, not always good. To Art she said, "Do you know why Jessica shot him in the car?"

"Well, sure, Gianna. He was with another guy."

"Yeah, I know that." According to the news story, Herb Addison had told police he ran when the woman pointed the gun.

"So, isn't it obvious?" Art asked.

"Spell it out for me, please," Gianna said tightly.

"They were, well, having sex. Alex was getting a blow job when Jessica appeared. She'd seen his car in the lot and walked over to it. It was late that night. And when she saw what was happening she took out this gun and the other guy got out of the car and ran like hell but Alex sat there trying to talk to Jessie, trying to explain..." Art trailed off, as if the realization had suddenly hit that there could be no way to explain that scenario to the most understanding of wives — and most certainly not to Jessica Brathwaite.

"Why these questions about Alex and Jessie?"

Gianna hesitated. Art deserved an answer, but she didn't want to reveal too much of what she was thinking. "I'm just trying to piece together some background material for an investigation —"

"Dear God," he breathed. "Oh Dear God, Gianna. I'd heard she was out but I never dreamed... it can't be possible, can it?"

Gianna literally heard her heart thud inside her chest. "You think Jessica has been released from St. Elizabeth's? When, Art? When?" Gianna clenched her fists. Jessica Brathwaite's name didn't show up on any release list ...

"I don't remember. A year ago maybe? I'm not really sure ..."

Art's response validated Gianna's suspicion but the central question remained: After almost twenty years of confinement, how would Jessica know Phil Tancil and Liz Grayson and Carolyn Green and the others? And even if she knew them, how could she know they were gay?

Gianna thanked Art and managed to grin as they performed their years-old ritual: He asks whether he'll see her Sunday; she responds that the time for miracles has passed; he reminds her that miracles occur every day, and she says then maybe Sunday's a good day for one. They both know that church isn't part of her program; but they both also know that in their respective lines of work, belief in miracles is sometimes the only way to get through a day.

Afterward, Gianna sat for a long moment, digesting all she'd just learned and seething at the incompetence that had denied her the knowledge that Jessica Brathwaite had been released from St. E's. She opened the report on recently released criminals and read the list name by name. Jessica Hendrix. Released from St. Elizabeth's Hospital on January 1, 1990, having spent 19 years and been declared no longer a danger to herself or others. And she winced when she read the notation in handwriting that she didn't recognize: *possible religious motivation ... no indication of sex motivation.* Forensics expert Asa Shehee's warning replayed itself in her head: "These crimes are not about sex, pure and simple."

She scanned the report, found what she sought: Jessica had been released to the care of the Presbyterian Home for Women in Wisconsin.

A pleasant conversation with an administrator there proved both helpful and frustrating. Yes, the woman said, Jessica had been there. She'd left after three weeks and no one had heard from her since.

"Could she be with her children?" Gianna asked.

"Oh, no, Lieutenant," said the gentle voice from the Presbyterian Women's Home. "His parents took the children after the ... after the incident. They were missionaries, you know, and lived abroad. And her family ... well, there was some embarrassment about the whole matter, as you might imagine."

Yes, Gianna could imagine. It was also becoming easier by the minute to imagine where Jessica had been since leaving Wisconsin.

"Money," Gianna said suddenly. "Where could she go without money?"

"Oh, that was no problem," said the gentle voice. "Her family was quite generous in that regard."

Yes, Gianna thought, embarrassment often breeds generosity. She checked her watch again: Barely eight-thirty. Over an hour before Eric would return. She was much too restless just to sit waiting for him. She toyed with the notion of calling him and trying to find out from Carolyn Green's husband whether his wife had known Jessica. She read over her notes from the newspaper article and her eyes focused on the Church Street address where Alex Brathwaite was killed. Wonder what's there now, she mused, even as she was writing a note for Eric to tell him what she'd learned and where she'd gone.

"I don't need this crap from you, Schuyler! You're supposed to be my friend!" Mimi snarled at Freddy and punched him in his huge bicep, but her heart wasn't in it. He'd rushed uptown to be with her after seeing the television news reports of Gianna's press conference, and though he was currently miserable because she was miserable — that was the kind of friends they were — he sided with Gianna.

"That one asshole all but accused Gianna of being a murderer, Mimi. And it's all because you wrote that story." Freddy snarled back.

"Five people are dead, Freddy, and the police —"

"I know that! One of them was a good friend of mine. But I don't think —" He stopped talking abruptly at the look on Mimi's face — a look of complete incomprehension. "What's wrong?"

"You said one of them was a friend?" She could barely speak.

"Yeah," Freddy said. "Joe Murray. Hell of a nice guy. But I didn't know until I read your story that his death was any more than a street mugging. That's what everybody was told."

"How did you know him? I never heard you mention him."

"He was involved for years with Alfie Cane, and you know Alfie's one of my best fr —"

"Joe Murray, Freddy," Mimi cut him off. "Tell me everything you know about Joe Murray."

Mimi sat on the sofa next to Freddy, insides

churning, as she listened to him describe Joe Murray's love affair with Alfonso "Alfie" Cane, another Washington Redskin, who, though he'd never held a press conference to announce it, was openly gay, and who wanted Joe Murray to be with him, to live with him as his lover.

"Joe wanted to but he just couldn't. You see, he loved his wife as much as he loved Alfie, and he was crazy about his kids. And his business was going great guns —"

Mimi interrupted. "Did he ever seek help, counseling?"

"Sure. I even drove him a couple of times to some kind of group session in a really tacky, run down building in southwest, down by the wharf —"

Mimi interrupted again, intense, taut. "In southwest? Not at Metro GALCO?"

Freddy shook his head and described a low-slung clapboard structure that backed up to one of the huge government parking lots and appeared totally out of place among the monstrous brick government office buildings. The hand-lettered sign in front identified it as the headquarters of some kind of Inter-Faith Ministry, and C.Y.K.A.S., the group that Joe Murray belonged to.

"Can You Keep A Secret. That's what it meant," Freddy said.

Mimi felt as bewildered as she knew she must look. Not once in her investigations had she heard of C.Y.K.A.S. and she'd checked every above ground and underground gay group in town; but she experienced the tingling sensation she always did when she knew she'd stumbled upon the truth in a story, when she'd found the heart of the beast she

161

was pursuing. She knew without question that whatever C.Y.K.A.S. was, it was at the heart of the murders of five people, all of whom had a secret to keep.

"Take me there, Freddy."

"Now?"

"Now."

She was already up and running, scurrying around collecting the tools of her trade: the small, automatic 35mm camera she used to take her own photos when necessary; press credentials on a chain around her neck but inside her sweater — unobtrusive but handy if necessary; a micro-cassette tape recorder; the ubiquitous tan reporter's notebook: and, as an afterthought, a small flashlight. She threw on her favorite jacket — ancient leather, bulky and blessed with pockets, into which she stuffed all the things she'd gathered, and opened the front door.

"Anytime tonight, Freddy," she intoned with dry sarcasm.

Freddy followed glumly, obviously more willing to confront an army of defensive tackles than whatever awaited them in some gloomy corner of southwest Washington.

Gianna drove uptown toward Church Street in an emotional fog. She could not free her mind of Mimi, of Mimi's eyes, of Mimi's touch, of her scent . . . When this is over, Gianna told herself, I can be with her again. Then she heard Mimi say, *Please don't do this Gianna,* and she wondered if she would ever again be held in those arms, ever again join with her to explore the far reaches of passion ... For the second time that night she put down the window and let the wintry night air dry her eyes.

She didn't need to check addresses on Church Street to know which house belonged to the Inner City Christian Ministry: It was the only one on the block not to have undergone the late 1970's phenomenon known as gentrification, a process that had transformed dozens of inner city poor and working-class neighborhoods into middle and upper-middle class havens of chic prosperity. No new, black, wrought iron fencing enclosed the scraggly yard, there was no sand-blasted brick, no new double-paned, energy efficient windows here. Even the hand-painted sign that welcomed all regardless of race, creed, gender, or sexual orientation had seen better days.

Gianna eased the Chevy into the tiny parking lot adjacent to the house — the parking lot where Alexander Brathwaite had been killed. Two cars were there, both old and battered and American, a thumb of the nose to the Saabs and Volvos and Toyotas and Nissans lining the street. Automatically, she wrote down the license plate numbers of both, and as she looked up she caught the fleeting motion of the front door closing ... and maybe, just maybe, she saw a person. Somebody who'd been around when Alexander Brathwaite was killed?

Gianna looked at the dashboard clock. Eric would soon be back at the office and reading the note she left for him, along with the Nexis newspaper article. She felt slightly and only momentarily guilty for not waiting for him and knew he'd understand.

After the second ring of the bell, Gianna heard

movement inside the house and a light went on in the foyer, followed by one on the outside wall of the house. She heard the safety chain on the door released, and the door opened slightly, but not enough for Gianna to see clearly who had opened it.

"Who is it?" asked a whispery voice.

"Lieutenant Anna Maglione, Metropolitan Police," Gianna answered, holding her photo-identification card toward the space in the door, and the door opened fully, permitting Gianna to see a shortish, slightly stooped, reddish-brown haired woman who, Gianna knew from the Nexus article, was now fifty-two years old. Despite the traumas of her life, she didn't look old and haggard, as Gianna expected, but she did seem tired beyond the world's ability to give her rest. She looked steadily, unblinkingly at Gianna with pale grey eyes and then, without a word, and without looking any further at the ID card Gianna continued to display, she raised her hands and Gianna was looking directly into the barrel of a .45 Colt automatic, the weapon she knew for certain had been used to kill Joe Murray, Tony delValle, Phil Tancil, Liz Grayson and Carolyn Green.

She looked from the gun to Jessica Hendrix, whose expression was unchanged, whose body was motionless. Jessica did not speak but she did motion for Gianna to enter. Gianna heard the door close, heard the locks set. She opened her mouth to speak but Jessica spoke first.

"Put your purse on the floor," Jessica commanded in her whispery voice, and Gianna obeyed, allowing the purse to slide off her shoulder and down her arm to the floor.

"Now take off your jacket," Jessica ordered and Gianna saw the woman's eyes narrow slightly as she hesitated, so she undid the buttons of her jacket with one hand and slid it off. She didn't need Jessica to tell her what to do with the holster and gun she wore strapped around her back and shoulders. She undid the straps and gently lowered the apparatus to the floor.

"Now turn around and walk straight through to the back of the house. Don't stop until you reach the back door."

Gianna followed orders, knowing that the best way to keep Jessica calm was to remain calm herself. She walked slowly down the dusty, ill-lit hallway, glancing left and right into rooms sparsely furnished in a style that had been outdated twenty years ago, and she wondered about the people who lived here, wondered whether Jessica had harmed them, thought she probably had. Still, Gianna felt no fear or panic until it was clear that the kitchen was not their final destination: Jessica propelled her out the back door, through the long, narrow yard so typical of Washington row houses, out to the alley, and to a car parked on a street a block away. Gianna was shivering, and not because her sweater was insufficient for the December night air. *Whoever said Jessica Hendrix was insane is a damn fool!* Jessica gave Gianna the keys and the order to open the passenger door, get in, and slide across to the driver's side.

"Jessica —" Gianna began.

"Shut up. Get on the 495 Beltway toward Maryland."

Gianna realized with a second rush of fear that

they must be headed for the home Jessica once shared with Alex. Why else would she go to Maryland? This woman, Gianna thought, is still firmly placed in 1971.

The rush hour traffic had thinned dramatically — there were fewer and fewer vehicles on the six lanes of expressway that had been a parking lot an hour ago. All the suburbanites were snug in their homes, warm and safe.

Gianna now felt full fear. She could imagine Eric's face when he found her car on Church Street, and then discovered her purse, jacket and gun on the hall floor . . .

X

Gianna drove up to a darkened, dowdy
ranch-style house on a quiet, tree-lined street and
thought that when the young minister and his
family had moved in all those years ago it would
have been considered quite a nice house. The brick
walkway that led to the front door was cracked and
worn with grass growing between the bricks, and the
house and yard were surrounded on both sides by
dense, overgrown yew bushes, which gave the place
a sinister look and feel. But then what could one
expect of a woman who'd spent nineteen years in

hell? That she'd come home and trim the hedges? What feelings live within a woman who'd lost her children — adults now, who'd been prevented from seeing their mother during her confinement and who hadn't wanted to see her after her release? Gianna wondered if Jessica had sat inside this house and plotted the brutal murders of five people.

There were no lights on the exterior of the house, but Gianna could see a faint glow from the rear, suggesting that Jessica Hendrix had expected to return here tonight. Gianna wasted a moment wishing she'd waited until the morning to discover what had become of the Inner City Ministry. Then she felt the full force of the realization that the woman intended to kill her and what hurt most was not that knowledge but the fact that if Jessica killed her the same way as the others, Mimi would know. . . .

For at least the twentieth time, Mimi rang Gianna's number, got the answering machine, and left a message. She'd been calling Gianna every thirty minutes since 1:00 a.m., after her visit to the C.Y.K.A.S. building. Gianna hadn't gone home last night. And she wasn't at the Cop Shop. Mimi rang the number again, primarily just to hear Gianna's voice. Then she called the Hate Crimes Unit yet again and heard yet again that Lt. Maglione was "not available." Mimi slammed down the phone with a snarl and turned to the notes she'd taken from her visit to C.Y.K.A.S.

The building was a rundown dump of a place,

dusty and airless. An old building directory listed some kind of religious ministry as the occupant, but there was no trace of such an organization. Only C.Y.K.A.S. existed, in a dingy office with a tartan plaid sofa, two tan Naugahyde chairs, and five metal folding chairs grouped around a battered card table. And a relatively new computer with a rudimentary program that Mimi accessed in two minutes and a file that held the names of at least two dozen people, including those of Joe Murray and Phil Tancil and Tony delValle and Liz Grayson and Carolyn Green... A file that also held Gianna's name, along with that of Dorothea Simpson, her former lover. Her former, *married* lover. Without a trace of a qualm, Mimi had made herself a backup copy of the file and then changed the file's name and locked it inside a password so that even the owner couldn't access it. Then she photographed the office and its contents, and placed tape on several of the desk drawers so she'd know if anyone entered the office between the time she'd left at midnight, and when she was able to tell Gianna. . . .

Where the hell was Gianna?

Mimi was supposed to be writing a follow-up story to the murders but she couldn't concentrate. She'd lost whatever excitement she'd felt about the discovery of C.Y.K.A.S. and its connection to all the victims. That excitement had been replaced by fear. Those other names in the computer — she'd have already called them under ordinary circumstances and coerced them into telling her who and what exactly C.Y.K.A.S. was. But at the moment, all she cared about was why she couldn't find Gianna, and that hollow thing called fear that was eating her insides, and made it impossible for her to write, to care about writing. For Gianna's name had been in that computer, and she'd deleted it to protect her, but now she was afraid — for Gianna and for herself.

Mimi jumped and snatched up the phone before the first ring was completed. Please be Gianna, she prayed silently.

"Patterson."

"I want to talk to the Montgomery Patterson who's been writing about the homosexual murders," said a whispery voice.

"Now's your chance. Talk to me," Mimi said, just this side of rude. *Where the hell was Gianna?*

"I thought you were a man."

"I'm not. What can I do for you?"

Her snarly tone didn't seem at all off-putting to the caller. "Maybe I can do something for you. Are you interested in writing about the police officer in charge of that investigation and how she's like the victims? That would make a good —"

"What are you talking about, Miss?" Mimi said rudely. The caller's voice irritated her.

"She's one of them, but she's in the closet, too."

Mimi heard a buzzing in her ears and then all the lights went out for a moment — a long moment — until she heard a voice calling to her in the phone which she still held.

"Hello? Hello? Are you still there? Hello?"

"Yes. I'm here. Who are you?" Recovering some of her wits, Mimi snatched open her desk drawer and rummaged around for her tape recorder and the illegal device that allowed her to record phone conversations without the knowledge of the other party.

"Never mind who I am, just answer my question. Are you interested in the story?" The voice was less wispy now.

Willing her hands to stop shaking, Mimi attached one end of the recording device to the phone, plugged the other into the tape recorder, and pressed the Record button, praying that the batteries still had some life as she sparred with her caller.

"If you're jerking me around, lady —"

"I'm not jerking you around. I promise you that."

"How can you be so sure about this cop? What's his name?"

"Don't play games with me, Miss Patterson. You know what cop and you know it's not a male. Do you want the story?"

"Yes, I want it. But I need to make sure you're not running a scam of some kind. And besides, I can't just write a story that says some cop is gay, taking your word for it. And suppose it's true? So what? Who cares? Lots of people are."

"Too many people are, that's the problem. People who shouldn't be. Good, decent people who have been corrupted by Satan and the evil he has spread throughout the world."

Mimi felt ill. "So, let me get this right." She prayed that her voice wouldn't tremble the way her body was. "You want me to write a story for the newspaper that says a cop who's investigating the murders of some gay people is also gay? And what else do I say after that? It's not exactly front page news." Mimi hoped that her off-hand sarcasm would anger the woman enough to keep her talking for a while. But the scheme backfired.

"Maybe by the time you write your story you can

say that she's dead, too, just like the others, because she will be."

Jessica slammed the phone down, stalked to where Gianna sat bound to a chair, and slammed a fist into her face. Gianna's head snapped back at the moment of impact — she had sensed the blow coming — so that she rode with the force of the blow, lessening its power. Which didn't mean it didn't hurt like hell.

It was the fifth time Jessica had hit her, and each time was associated with anger. And when she was angry Jessica became the insane person that almost twenty years in St. E's had failed to cure. Come to think of it, Gianna mused, it was hard to imagine anybody being cured of insanity inside an insane asylum. The whole notion was insane! She laughed to herself but it must not have been only to herself for Jessica turned on her with a look of pure hatred and she took the butt of the gun and hit her in the right bicep. Gianna hadn't anticipated that one and had not flexed the muscle to absorb the impact and she groaned as the pain shot through her body.

"I'm glad you hurt," Jessica hissed. "You deserve to hurt."

"Why, Jessica? What have I done to you?"

"You're immoral." Jessica spat the words at her. "You live against the laws of God. You live in sin," she huffed, turning to the Bible that she read endlessly.

"But I haven't killed anybody," Gianna said

evenly and then recoiled in horror as Jessica whirled around, her face twisted beyond recognition, suffused with anger and hatred and pain.

"*Yes you did!* You killed my Alex."

"Jessica. You killed Alex." She kept her voice controlled and steeled herself for the blow that did not come.

"That's what they say but they're liars, infidels. Perverts."

"But you did kill the others, didn't you, Jessica? Joe and Tony and Liz and Phil and Carolyn? You killed them, too, Jessica?"

"Because they were going to leave, to go away, to go live in sin. Like Alex wanted to." Jessica's voice took on a sing-song quality and her body relaxed and she drifted about the room as if floating in a daze, an exercise accommodated by the lack of furniture: Gianna was tied to one of the room's two chairs, an armless high-backed side chair, and Jessica's Bible occupied the other — a floral print wing chair. The only other furniture was a small table that held the phone.

Jessica stood in the middle of the floor, swaying gently, eyes closed, but facing Gianna. "Alex said he couldn't live with me and the children until he discovered the truth of himself. At first I didn't understand. I thought he wanted to live at the church, like the Catholics. But then I realized he meant to live with a man named Carlos, to live with him like he lived with me. I told him that was a sin against God but he said that God loved us no matter who we loved." She paused to pick up her Bible, but she still looked and acted dream-like.

Gianna wondered what kind of medication

sustained a person after almost twenty years of confinement to a mental institution where drugs were a daily necessity.

"I tried to help them. I really did," Jessica whispered.

"You tried to help who, Jessica?" Gianna asked softly.

"All of them, so they wouldn't have to die. But they were like Alex. They wanted to live in sin but I made them all pray and confess their sins. God will forgive them but not you . . ." She trailed off and resumed her wandering around the room.

"Jessica, why do you want to kill me?" Gianna sensed Jessica's mood shifting and she wanted to keep her talking, to get as much of a confession as possible. She wouldn't allow herself to worry about living long enough to tell anybody.

"Because you're like them. A shameless sinner."

"It's not a sin to love, Jessica."

"You break the laws of God and man. You disrespect the sanctity of marriage and the blessings of children when you interfere with husband and wife."

"But I don't have a husband, Jessica, or children. I'm not leaving anybody, and the woman I love doesn't have a husband . . ."

"You're a liar!" Jessica snapped at her and Gianna tensed as she realized the dream-like trance had ended.

"I'm telling you the truth —" Gianna's head snapped back with the force of the slap but she met and held Jessica's eyes. It was her only hope — Jessica attacked more often and hit harder when she sensed weakness. But inside Gianna fought a wave

174

of pure terror. Jessica was convinced she was lying and Gianna had no idea why.

Finally Jessica turned away to seek the solace of her Bible, and Gianna looked toward the heavily draperied windows through which she could see nothing except increasing darkness. It had been dark when she arrived here last night at about 10:30 and it was getting dark again. She'd been here, she calculated, sixteen hours. She watched Jessica's lips silently move as she read her Bible, and wondered idly whether the other parts of this house were as barren as this room. She wondered how Jessica knew she was a lesbian. She wondered why Jessica called her a liar. She wondered what Eric was doing. She wondered what Mimi was doing. She wondered whether she'd live to find out. And for the first time ever she wondered whether it might truly be better for all homosexuals and lesbians to exit the closet. What had Cedric said? Keeping secrets is different from keeping privacy. If Joe and Phil and Liz and Tony and Carolyn hadn't kept their secret they'd likely be alive. And she wouldn't be tied to a chair facing death, worried about keeping her own secret.

Mimi squeezed her eyes shut and massaged her temples, mad as hell and sorrier than shit that she'd voluntarily come to police headquarters to share what she'd discovered about C.Y.K.A.S. with Gianna's second-in-command at Hate Crimes. She'd had a fierce battle with Tyler about it — he hadn't wanted to reveal anything to the cops — but she'd been motivated by her fear for Gianna. What if the cops

175

didn't know what she knew... What if they didn't find Gianna in time...

Eric Ashby had been badgering her for almost an hour, had made her repeat over and over and over again, despite the fact that she'd given him the tape recording, the details of her call from the woman they now knew was Jessica Hendrix. He'd made her tell him again and again of her conversation with Freddy Schuyler explaining C.Y.K.A.S. And he took particular joy in having her replay how she broke into the C.Y.K.A.S. office in southwest last night — Christ, it felt like an eternity ago — and then how she broke into the computer and deciphered enough of the C.Y.K.A.S. file to come up with an address of a house in suburban Maryland. And then he asked her again why she thought Jessica Hendrix planned to kill Gianna.

"You heard the tape yourself. She said she'd kill her." She could not tell Ashby that Gianna had come to Jessica Hendrix's attention because of Gianna's relationship to Dorothea Simpson, Gianna's married ex-lover, who had been listed on Hendrix's computer as a member of C.Y.K.A.S. To reveal this information was to out Gianna, and this Mimi refused to do.

Mimi showed her disgust with him by turning away and studying the enlarged photographs of the murdered Carolyn Green that hung next to those of the other victims. Carolyn was the only one whose face Mimi had not memorized, the only one whose photo she did not have. She remembered what Gianna had said that night, overcome by anger and fatigue: "She looked like you, Mimi..."

This was her first time inside the Think Tank and she absorbed every detail of the room, imagining

Gianna at work here, willing every one of her senses to call up Gianna, to place her in the here and now. Gianna, who'd disappeared sixteen, maybe seventeen hours ago, whom Jessica Hendrix had threatened to kill. Mimi was weak from lack of sleep or food, was kept alert by fear. Suppose Jessica had already...

The door opened and Tyler — whom she'd forgotten about — came in, followed by the Chief of Police. Eric scowled but Mimi brightened immediately. "Listen, Chief," she began.

Eric pounded the table. "Goddammit, the Chief's not conducting this interview, I am!"

"I know it, Detective," Mimi said wearily. "But you seem to have trouble hearing. I've answered that same question in exactly the same way more times than I can count."

"And by God you'll keep answering if I keep asking!"

Tyler cleared his throat. "No, Detective, she won't. We're here voluntarily. We have turned over confidential notes to you, we have given you a tape recording. . . ."

"Which you illegally obtained," Eric snarled.

"The fact is, Detective, it's more than you had. And now we've told you where Jessica Hendrix is most likely holding your Lieutenant and your response is to threaten my reporter? Well, sir, try this on for size: as of this moment, Miss Patterson will say not another word to you. She will not answer another question. And if I leave this room again it will be to call the company lawyers and by the time they finish filing motions it'll take you a week to dig yourself from under the paper. Do I make myself clear?"

177

Mimi had never heard Tyler so icy and she was impressed. She also liked it that he called her "his" reporter. She must be more exhausted than she knew, but she was now also angry, thanks to Tyler's timely intervention.

"Listen, Ashby, you little shit. I don't care what you think about me. Right now your boss's life is in jeopardy and I'd think you'd care more about saving her than wasting time hassling me."

The Chief cleared his throat and gave her a hard look. "We appreciate your cooperation, Miss Patterson," he said more rapid-fire than usual and rocking on his toes, "and nobody wastes time around here. I'm on my way to Montgomery County. Care to join me for a chopper ride?"

The blue jump-suited, flack-jacketed Montgomery County SWAT Team scurried under the shrubbery and between the houses and behind the cars like so many rats, now visible, now the merest hint of a shadow, now gone. Mimi sat inside an FBI car with Tyler and his friend Don. At the moment, she was thoroughly disgusted with the D.C. police. But she could see Eric Ashby's red hair bristling in the darkness, the tension in him crackling like electricity. He obviously was not accustomed to inaction, to hanging back waiting for other cops to act. But for the moment, Gianna belonged to the Montgomery County SWAT Team, not to Eric and the Hate Crimes team, and all they could do — all any of them could do — was wait.

Mimi knew from experience that cops exude a

different energy when one of their own is in danger. Not that they don't exert themselves in defense of the ordinary citizenry; but one cop in danger imperils them all and they respond as if failure to save their comrade signals their collective inability to save themselves. The same tension that she could see in Eric, in the Chief, she could see and feel in Don inside the car.

Then she heard before she saw anything the simultaneous explosion of splintering wood and shattering glass as SWAT team members crashed through doors and windows and into the house. Then there was a moment of pure silence then screams then shots and everything within Mimi broke, collapsed, and she jumped out of the car and ran toward the house before Tyler and Don could stop her. She ran, her insides boiling with fear and pain, and when Don and Eric grabbed her she fought them, struggling blindly, in vain, until Tyler put his arms around her and held her with more power than she would have believed he possessed. Then he was yelling for her to look! Look! And she saw Gianna being led, being half-carried from the house by two huge SWAT-ters and the three of them safely surrounded by half a dozen others. Weak, exhausted, injured somehow, though Mimi didn't know exactly how, but alive and not shot.

"Tyler, please let me go —"

"You can't, Mimi, not now. You know they won't let you get close to her, not now."

"But I just want to see her ..."

"She's okay, Mimi. She's fine. She's walking ..."

And at that moment Gianna saw Mimi, they saw each other, and Mimi broke from Tyler and ran toward her only to be intercepted by Eric who warned her that the SWAT Team was still on full alert and would probably shoot her if she got any closer.

But then Gianna smiled at her, or tried to, and Mimi ceased her struggle with Eric. "You can let me go now, Detective. I won't do anything."

Mimi's eyes stayed glued to Gianna, who was led by the two bulky SWAT team members to an ambulance, where two paramedics gently lowered her onto a stretcher and immediately began to check her. Mimi's eyes never wavered as the Chief hurried to Gianna, leaned over her, said something that made Gianna attempt a smile and Mimi could tell by the way the smile stopped in mid-attempt that something was wrong with Gianna's face. The chief tousled Gianna's hair as if she were a wayward child and the tears sprang to Mimi's eyes and she allowed them to fall as the Chief hustled away and the paramedics lifted the stretcher and enclosed Gianna inside the ambulance.

And that was when Mimi became aware of the second ambulance and the second team of paramedics and the second stretcher — the one being rolled, with no sense of urgency, up the walkway to the recently liberated house. Mimi sought out Tyler, saw him sprinting toward her, knew what he wanted from her.

"You have your camera?" he panted.

She patted her pocket, hauled out the small camera, and quickly followed him to the house, checking the camera's settings en route. As her reporter's brain began functioning again, she realized the meaning of all the gunfire: If Gianna and all the

180

SWAT team members were still alive, Jessica was not. She readied the camera though she knew it would be a long while before the body was removed.

"Miss Patterson?" She turned to see Eric Ashby.

"Will you answer one question for me?"

Mimi shrugged. "Depends on the question."

"Who's Dorothea?" he asked.

"Dorothea is a bleeping idiot," Mimi said, with feeling.

They worked in a small, sparsely furnished room in the basement of Montgomery County General Hospital. Mimi didn't want to think about why the room smelled vaguely of formaldehyde because she was having trouble enough keeping her mind on the task at hand. The room was private and it was quiet and that's what she needed. Tyler tapped away at the keys of the laptop computer as Mimi dictated the story to him in a fierce jumble of words that sometimes made sense and sometimes did not. Tyler, a reporter for more years than he was an editor, would know instinctively when and how to organize, correct, add to, delete from, the tale Mimi spun of how and why Jessica Hendrix murdered five people and would have made Police Lieutenant Maglione her sixth victim if not for the swift and precise action of the Montgomery County SWAT Team.

Since Tyler occupied the only chair, Mimi paced. She nibbled at an apple she'd gotten from the cafeteria; Tyler had virtually inhaled the burger and fries she'd brought him and was eyeing her banana greedily. She didn't care. She was forcing the apple down only because she knew she should. The harsh fluorescence of the overhead light hurt her eyes. She had a monstrous headache. And she wanted to see Gianna who was somewhere in this building.

"How do we deal with the fact that a police Lieutenant almost became a victim when all the others were gay?" Tyler asked.

"Because she was getting too close, Tyler, and that's the truth. She knew that Jessica Hendrix was the killer and was closing in on her."

"But that's only half the truth, Mimi."

"I will not expose her Tyler, and that's final."

"You're obligated to report the entire story."

"Then I'm also obligated to report the assistance and involvement of my gay editor and his gay FBI agent boyfriend who just happens to have a wife and two kids. Right, Tyler?"

He muttered something under his breath that Mimi didn't hear but could well imagine and typed rapidly for several minutes without speaking. He stilled his fingers long enough to peel the banana.

"You and Gianna stumbled onto the Hendrix woman independent of each other?" he asked, chewing. Mimi nodded assent and was startled when Tyler said testily, "Well? I'm waiting."

"Waiting for what?" She was remembering how and why it happened that she and Gianna had ended up on divergent courses of investigation, ended up away and apart from each other and with Gianna in danger.

"For you to tell me how you learned that Jessica Hendrix was the killer," he said in a tone that suggested she was the one who'd spent the last twenty years in St. Elizabeth's.

And as Mimi explained about Freddy and Joe Murray, about Calvin Cobbs and the "funny little lady" who had haunted the Metro GALCO seminars, the story emerged of a hate-filled, calculated plan to destroy gay people who, in the mind of Jessica Hendrix, would, if permitted, destroy those who loved them.

"I don't understand. How'd that work, Mimi?"

"She'd attend the out-of-the-closet classes for married people, always masquerading as a woman too afraid to open her closet door. Then she'd insinuate herself with others like herself — Liz Grayson, Phil Tancil, Joe Murray, Tony delValle, Carolyn Green — all too afraid to be publicly gay. Then, according to Freddy who says Joe Murray told him, she advocated the formation of a group dedicated to keeping their secret, to keeping their families, to keeping their jobs — in short, to having it all."

She stopped talking as she remembered Calvin Cobbs, persuasive, logical, rational, loving, urging the people in the seminar to reveal their secret, to come out of the closet, to tell the truth. Jessica must have been a relief to them, telling them exactly what they wanted to hear.

"Can You Keep A Secret. That's all any of them ever wanted to do. It's really quite simple when you think of it," she said wearily, fatigue once more descending upon her.

"But then why kill them? What was the point?"

"With Jessica dead, we can't be sure, Tyler, but I think the people who died were on the verge of making a decision — a choice — and I think the choice was not to Jessica's liking. Sources tell me

Carolyn Green had already told her husband she was leaving. And don't you dare write that!" she yelled at him as his fingers sped over the keys.

"So if they wouldn't keep their own secrets, she'd help them do it," Tyler mused sadly, shaking his head. "And now everyone knows their secret anyway." He typed quickly and silently for a few moments then, with a puzzled look, asked, "So how come she was outing Schuyler if keeping secrets was her mission?"

"Tyler, the woman was insane. Don't look for logic."

"Okay. So, all that's left is the background history on the Hendrix woman and a statement from the cops. And of course I'd dearly love to know the path that led your Gianna to Hendrix..."

In a tight voice Mimi said, "The Hendrix backgrounder is in my computer at the office. The password is —"

Tyler, in a flash of pure irritation, complained, "I don't see why you can't come back to the paper for just an hour."

"I'm not leaving her, I told you," Mimi snapped at him.

"Dammit, Patterson, their debriefing of her could go on all night. And that's only after the doctors say it's okay for them to question her. She was hurt, you saw that —"

Mimi cut him off with a cry of pain so intense she, too, could have been physically assaulted. "Fire me, Tyler, kill me, I don't care. I'm not leaving her."

His sigh of resignation coincided with the knock and the opening of the door. A drained and exhausted Eric Ashby stuck his head in, nodded at Tyler and said to Mimi in a tight, hoarse voice, "Can I see you for a moment, Miss Patterson?"

Alarmed, Mimi crossed quickly to the door and followed him out. He strode down the hall to a bank of elevators and pressed the button to the one marked Hospital Personnel Only. He turned to her as they waited.

"First off, I owe you an apology. I didn't realize you and Anna...the Lieutenant...that you were, ah..."

"You don't owe me anything. You were doing your job."

"It's just that we're very protective of her."

"And I'm very grateful for that," Mimi said honestly.

"I hope I haven't put my foot in it, but Anna... the Lieutenant, asked me to drive her home and I told her you were here but she didn't want to ask you..."

"They're not keeping her overnight?" Mimi asked quickly.

"She won't stay," Eric responded ruefully and they shared a look that almost became a smile as Mimi realized that he, as well as she, understood the stubborn nature of Lt. Maglione.

"By the way, Detective. You look like bloody hell."

"Then we must be related, Miss Patterson," he said as they exited the elevator, this time sharing a real smile.

Mimi followed Eric to an unmarked door which he opened with a key and then stepped aside to let her enter. It was a small room, barely large enough for the bed, chair, toilet and basin it held. Gianna was sunk back into the chair, feet outstretched, head back, eyes closed.

Eric closed the door and Mimi heard it lock. She took several steps toward Gianna and was almost upon her when the hazel eyes opened — eyes no longer bright and clear but filled with pain and fatigue and loss and grief. A deep bruise showed purplish-black on her right cheekbone. Mimi knelt before her, put her head in her lap, and wept.

Gianna stroked her hair and caressed her neck for a long moment before taking her face in her hands and raising her head.

"Don't, darling, please . . ." Gianna whispered.

"How can you call me that?" Mimi hurled the words at her.

"Easily. I love you."

"I almost got you killed." Mimi pulled her face and body away from Gianna and jumped to her feet.

"Eric says you saved my life, that you figured out where she'd taken me —"

Mimi cut her off with a painful cry. "It was my fault you were there! If I hadn't written that story . . . That's what set her off and made her target you."

"Is that what you think?" Gianna asked incredulously. "That you . . . that what happened between us somehow is responsible for what that poor, insane woman did?" Gianna waited for a response that was too slow coming so she prodded, "Is that it, Mimi? Tell me."

"Yes," Mimi said almost inaudibly. She was washing her face in the sink and shivering as much from the frigid water as from the gradual release of the emotion pent up inside her.

"Well, you're wrong, and you'll get rid of that notion quickly unless you want to put distance between us."

"Unless I want distance between us? You're the one who put the distance between us!" Mimi yelled the words and she threw the balled-up paper towels she'd used to dry her face at Gianna who caught them with a wry grin.

"You were right and I was wrong. I had eighteen hours to think about nothing but how wrong I was to send you away, to walk away from you. It was dumb. It was unnecessary. And I'm sorry."

Mimi went to her and knelt down beside her. "But you thought I would betray you or your investigation."

"I never thought that. Never. I was afraid of myself, Mimi, afraid that I couldn't love you well enough and do my job well enough at the same time. And for the first time in my life I found that I resented the job and that scared me."

Gianna seemed about to say more but shook her head and turned her eyes to Mimi.

Mimi kissed them, gently, first one and then the other, wanting to kiss away the hurt and the pain. She kissed the bruise under the right eye, afraid to know how it came to be there, and she kissed her mouth, softly, gently, and then she collapsed in her arms and wept again and out tumbled the fear that had been locked inside her — the fear that she'd lost Gianna forever and the certain knowledge that life with such pain would be impossible, and Gianna held and rocked her and whispered to her until the sobs abated, then Gianna wiped her face with the towels that had been hurled in anger just moments before.

"What about your story?" Gianna asked softly.

"Tyler's working on it downstairs in the basement. We're almost finished."

"You have everything you need? A statement from the police?"

Gianna wore her Lieutenant's face so Mimi knew she was serious but she wasn't sure how to respond. Haltingly she asked, "You mean a statement from you?"

And when Gianna nodded Mimi laughed out loud, through her tears, imagining Tyler's glee at being able to interview the police Lieutenant who'd solved the city's first serial murder case in two decades by almost becoming a victim herself. He'd be so pleased with himself he'd become his usual obnoxious self before the night was over.

"Let's go find Tyler. He'll be thrilled."

"Tell me something before we go?"

"What? Anything." Mimi looked into her eyes.

"Tell me you love me," Gianna whispered.

"I love you."

"Tell me you'll take me away from this madness, someplace we can't be found for at least a week."

"I'll take you to a cabin in Garrett County, a place where if it snows no one will be able to get in and we can't get out. We'll look out onto a massive dark blue lake and into thick woods beyond where you can see deer, and champagne by the case is stacked up in the pantry, and the fireplace logs are three feet long and will burn for hours. And there's a hot tub on the deck."

"Tell me you'll take me tomorrow."
"Freddy will fly us up in his plane."
"Tell me you love me again."
"I love you again. And again. Forever."

A few of the publications of
THE NAIAD PRESS, INC.
P.O. Box 10543 • Tallahassee, Florida 32302
Phone (904) 539-5965
Toll-Free Order Number: 1-800-533-1973
Mail orders welcome. Please include 15% postage.

MICHAELA by Sarah Aldridge. 256 pp. A "Sarah Aldridge" romance. ISBN 1-56280-055-8 $10.95

KEEPING SECRETS by Penny Mickelbury. 208 pp. A Gianna Maglione Mystery. First in a series. ISBN 1-56280-052-3   9.95

THE ROMANTIC NAIAD edited by Katherine V. Forrest & Barbara Grier. 336 pp. Love stories by Naiad Press women. ISBN 1-56280-054-X   14.95

UNDER MY SKIN by Jaye Maiman. 336 pp. A Robin Miller mystery. 3rd in a series. ISBN 1-56280-049-3.   10.95

STAY TOONED by Rhonda Dicksion. 144 pp. Cartoons — 1st collection since *Lesbian Survival Manual.* ISBN 1-56280-045-0   9.95

CAR POOL by Karin Kallmaker. 272pp. Lesbians on wheels and then some! ISBN 1-56280-048-5   9.95

NOT TELLING MOTHER: STORIES FROM A LIFE by Diane Salvatore. 176 pp. Her 3rd novel. ISBN 1-56280-044-2   9.95

GOBLIN MARKET by Lauren Wright Douglas. 240pp. A Caitlin Reece Mystery. 5th in a series. ISBN 1-56280-047-7   9.95

LONG GOODBYES by Nikki Baker. 256 pp. A Virginia Kelly mystery. 3rd in a series. ISBN 1-56280-042-6   9.95

FRIENDS AND LOVERS by Jackie Calhoun. 224 pp. Mid-western Lesbian lives and loves. ISBN 1-56280-041-8   9.95

THE CAT CAME BACK by Hilary Mullins. 208 pp. Highly praised Lesbian novel. ISBN 1-56280-040-X   9.95

BEHIND CLOSED DOORS by Robbi Sommers. 192 pp. Hot, erotic short stories. ISBN 1-56280-039-6   9.95

CLAIRE OF THE MOON by Nicole Conn. 192 pp. See the movie — read the book! ISBN 1-56280-038-8   10.95

SILENT HEART by Claire McNab. 192 pp. Exotic Lesbian romance. ISBN 1-56280-036-1   9.95

HAPPY ENDINGS by Kate Brandt. 272 pp. Intimate conversations with Lesbian authors. ISBN 1-56280-050-7   10.95

THE SPY IN QUESTION by Amanda Kyle Williams. 256 pp. 4th
Madison McGuire.   ISBN 1-56280-037-X   9.95

SAVING GRACE by Jennifer Fulton. 240 pp. Adventure and
romantic entanglement.   ISBN 1-56280-051-5   9.95

THE YEAR SEVEN by Molleen Zanger. 208 pp. Women surviving
in a new world.   ISBN 1-56280-034-5   9.95

CURIOUS WINE by Katherine V. Forrest. 176 pp. Tenth
Anniversary Edition. The most popular contemporary Lesbian
love story.   ISBN 1-56280-053-1   9.95

CHAUTAUQUA by Catherine Ennis. 192 pp. Exciting, romantic
adventure.   ISBN 1-56280-032-9   9.95

A PROPER BURIAL by Pat Welch. 192 pp. A Helen Black
mystery. 3rd in a series.   ISBN 1-56280-033-7   9.95

SILVERLAKE HEAT: A Novel of Suspense by Carol Schmidt.
240 pp. Rhonda is as hot as Laney's dreams.   ISBN 1-56280-031-0   9.95

LOVE, ZENA BETH by Diane Salvatore. 224 pp. The most talked
about lesbian novel of the nineties!   ISBN 1-56280-030-2   9.95

A DOORYARD FULL OF FLOWERS by Isabel Miller. 160 pp.
Stories incl. 2 sequels to *Patience and Sarah.*   ISBN 1-56280-029-9   9.95

MURDER BY TRADITION by Katherine V. Forrest. 288 pp. A
Kate Delafield Mystery. 4th in a series.   ISBN 1-56280-002-7   9.95

THE EROTIC NAIAD edited by Katherine V. Forrest & Barbara Grier.
224 pp. Love stories by Naiad Press authors.   ISBN 1-56280-026-4   12.95

DEAD CERTAIN by Claire McNab. 224 pp. A Carol Ashton
mystery. 5th in a series.   ISBN 1-56280-027-2   9.95

CRAZY FOR LOVING by Jaye Maiman. 320 pp. A Robin Miller
mystery. 2nd in a series.   ISBN 1-56280-025-6   9.95

STONEHURST by Barbara Johnson. 176 pp. Passionate regency
romance.   ISBN 1-56280-024-8   9.95

INTRODUCING AMANDA VALENTINE by Rose Beecham.
256 pp. An Amanda Valentine Mystery. First in a series.
                                          ISBN 1-56280-021-3   9.95

UNCERTAIN COMPANIONS by Robbi Sommers. 204 pp.
Steamy, erotic novel.   ISBN 1-56280-017-5   9.95

A TIGER'S HEART by Lauren W. Douglas. 240 pp. A Caitlin
Reece mystery. 4th in a series.   ISBN 1-56280-018-3   9.95

PAPERBACK ROMANCE by Karin Kallmaker. 256 pp. A
delicious romance.   ISBN 1-56280-019-1   9.95

MORTON RIVER VALLEY by Lee Lynch. 304 pp. Lee Lynch at
her best!   ISBN 1-56280-016-7   9.95

THE LAVENDER HOUSE MURDER by Nikki Baker. 224 pp. A
Virginia Kelly Mystery. 2nd in a series.   ISBN 1-56280-012-4   9.95

PASSION BAY by Jennifer Fulton. 224 pp. Passionate romance,
virgin beaches, tropical skies.　　　　ISBN 1-56280-028-0　　9.95

STICKS AND STONES by Jackie Calhoun. 208 pp. Contemporary
lesbian lives and loves.　　　　ISBN 1-56280-020-5　　9.95

DELIA IRONFOOT by Jeane Harris. 192 pp. Adventure for Delia
and Beth in the Utah mountains.　　　　ISBN 1-56280-014-0　　9.95

UNDER THE SOUTHERN CROSS by Claire McNab. 192 pp.
Romantic nights Down Under.　　　　ISBN 1-56280-011-6　　9.95

RIVERFINGER WOMEN by Elana Nachman/Dykewomon.
208 pp. Classic Lesbian/feminist novel.　　　ISBN 1-56280-013-2　　8.95

A CERTAIN DISCONTENT by Cleve Boutell. 240 pp. A unique
coterie of women.　　　　ISBN 1-56280-009-4　　9.95

GRASSY FLATS by Penny Hayes. 256 pp. Lesbian romance in
the '30s.　　　　ISBN 1-56280-010-8　　9.95

A SINGULAR SPY by Amanda K. Williams. 192 pp. 3rd Madison
McGuire.　　　　ISBN 1-56280-008-6　　8.95

THE END OF APRIL by Penny Sumner. 240 pp. A Victoria Cross
Mystery. First in a series.　　　　ISBN 1-56280-007-8　　8.95

A FLIGHT OF ANGELS by Sarah Aldridge. 240 pp. Romance set at
the National Gallery of Art　　　　ISBN 1-56280-001-9　　9.95

HOUSTON TOWN by Deborah Powell. 208 pp. A Hollis Carpenter
mystery. Second in a series.　　　　ISBN 1-56280-006-X　　8.95

KISS AND TELL by Robbi Sommers. 192 pp. Scorching stories by
the author of *Pleasures*.　　　　ISBN 1-56280-005-1　　9.95

STILL WATERS by Pat Welch. 208 pp. A Helen Black mystery.
2nd in a series.　　　　ISBN 0-941483-97-5　　9.95

TO LOVE AGAIN by Evelyn Kennedy. 208 pp. Wildly
romantic love story.　　　　ISBN 0-941483-85-1　　9.95

IN THE GAME by Nikki Baker. 192 pp. A Virginia Kelly
mystery. First in a series.　　　　ISBN 01-56280-004-3　　9.95

AVALON by Mary Jane Jones. 256 pp. A Lesbian Arthurian
romance.　　　　ISBN 0-941483-96-7　　9.95

STRANDED by Camarin Grae. 320 pp. Entertaining, riveting
adventure.　　　　ISBN 0-941483-99-1　　9.95

THE DAUGHTERS OF ARTEMIS by Lauren Wright Douglas.
240 pp. A Caitlin Reece mystery. 3rd in a series.
　　　　ISBN 0-941483-95-9　　9.95

CLEARWATER by Catherine Ennis. 176 pp. Romantic secrets
of a small Louisiana town.　　　　ISBN 0-941483-65-7　　8.95

THE HALLELUJAH MURDERS by Dorothy Tell. 176 pp. A Poppy
Dillworth mystery. 2nd in a series.　　ISBN 0-941483-88-6　　8.95

ZETA BASE by Judith Alguire. 208 pp. Lesbian triangle
on a future Earth.   ISBN 0-941483-94-0   9.95

SECOND CHANCE by Jackie Calhoun. 256 pp. Contemporary
Lesbian lives and loves.   ISBN 0-941483-93-2   9.95

BENEDICTION by Diane Salvatore. 272 pp. Striking,
contemporary romantic novel.   ISBN 0-941483-90-8   9.95

CALLING RAIN by Karen Marie Christa Minns. 240 pp.
Spellbinding, erotic love story   ISBN 0-941483-87-8   9.95

BLACK IRIS by Jeane Harris. 192 pp. Caroline's hidden past . . .
                                            ISBN 0-941483-68-1   8.95

TOUCHWOOD by Karin Kallmaker. 240 pp. Loving, May/
December romance.   ISBN 0-941483-76-2   9.95

BAYOU CITY SECRETS by Deborah Powell. 224 pp. A Hollis
Carpenter mystery. First in a series.   ISBN 0-941483-91-6   9.95

COP OUT by Claire McNab. 208 pp. A Carol Ashton mystery.
4th in a series.   ISBN 0-941483-84-3   9.95

LODESTAR by Phyllis Horn. 224 pp. Romantic, fast-moving
adventure.   ISBN 0-941483-83-5   8.95

THE BEVERLY MALIBU by Katherine V. Forrest. 288 pp. A
Kate Delafield Mystery. 3rd in a series.   ISBN 0-941483-48-7   9.95

THAT OLD STUDEBAKER by Lee Lynch. 272 pp. Andy's affair
with Regina and her attachment to her beloved car.
                                            ISBN 0-941483-82-7   9.95

PASSION'S LEGACY by Lori Paige. 224 pp. Sarah is swept into
the arms of Augusta Pym in this delightful historical romance.
                                            ISBN 0-941483-81-9   8.95

THE PROVIDENCE FILE by Amanda Kyle Williams. 256 pp.
Second Madison McGuire   ISBN 0-941483-92-4   8.95

I LEFT MY HEART by Jaye Maiman. 320 pp. A Robin Miller
Mystery. First in a series.   ISBN 0-941483-72-X   9.95

THE PRICE OF SALT by Patricia Highsmith (writing as Claire
Morgan). 288 pp. Classic lesbian novel, first issued in 1952 . . .
acknowledged by its author under her own, very famous, name.
                                            ISBN 1-56280-003-5   9.95

SIDE BY SIDE by Isabel Miller. 256 pp. From beloved author of
Patience and Sarah.   ISBN 0-941483-77-0   9.95

STAYING POWER: LONG TERM LESBIAN COUPLES
by Susan E. Johnson. 352 pp. Joys of coupledom.
                                            ISBN 0-941-483-75-4   12.95

SLICK by Camarin Grae. 304 pp. Exotic, erotic adventure.
                                            ISBN 0-941483-74-6   9.95

NINTH LIFE by Lauren Wright Douglas. 256 pp. A Caitlin
Reece mystery. 2nd in a series.   ISBN 0-941483-50-9   8.95

PLAYERS by Robbi Sommers. 192 pp. Sizzling, erotic novel.
ISBN 0-941483-73-8   9.95

MURDER AT RED ROOK RANCH by Dorothy Tell. 224 pp.
A Poppy Dillworth mystery. 1st in a series.   ISBN 0-941483-80-0   8.95

LESBIAN SURVIVAL MANUAL by Rhonda Dicksion.
112 pp. Cartoons!   ISBN 0-941483-71-1   8.95

A ROOM FULL OF WOMEN by Elisabeth Nonas. 256 pp.
Contemporary Lesbian lives.   ISBN 0-941483-69-X   9.95

PRIORITIES by Lynda Lyons 288 pp. Science fiction with
a twist.   ISBN 0-941483-66-5   8.95

THEME FOR DIVERSE INSTRUMENTS by Jane Rule. 208
pp. Powerful romantic lesbian stories.   ISBN 0-941483-63-0   8.95

LESBIAN QUERIES by Hertz & Ertman. 112 pp. The questions
you were too embarrassed to ask.   ISBN 0-941483-67-3   8.95

CLUB 12 by Amanda Kyle Williams. 288 pp. Espionage thriller
featuring a lesbian agent!   ISBN 0-941483-64-9   8.95

DEATH DOWN UNDER by Claire McNab. 240 pp. A Carol
Ashton mystery. 3rd in a series.   ISBN 0-941483-39-8   9.95

MONTANA FEATHERS by Penny Hayes. 256 pp. Vivian and
Elizabeth find love in frontier Montana.   ISBN 0-941483-61-4   8.95

CHESAPEAKE PROJECT by Phyllis Horn. 304 pp. Jessie &
Meredith in perilous adventure.   ISBN 0-941483-58-4   8.95

LIFESTYLES by Jackie Calhoun. 224 pp. Contemporary Lesbian
lives and loves.   ISBN 0-941483-57-6   9.95

VIRAGO by Karen Marie Christa Minns. 208 pp. Darsen has
chosen Ginny.   ISBN 0-941483-56-8   8.95

WILDERNESS TREK by Dorothy Tell. 192 pp. Six women on
vacation learning ''new'' skills.   ISBN 0-941483-60-6   8.95

MURDER BY THE BOOK by Pat Welch. 256 pp. A Helen
Black Mystery. First in a series.   ISBN 0-941483-59-2   9.95

LESBIANS IN GERMANY by Lillian Faderman & B. Eriksson.
128 pp. Fiction, poetry, essays.   ISBN 0-941483-62-2   8.95

THERE'S SOMETHING I'VE BEEN MEANING TO TELL
YOU Ed. by Loralee MacPike. 288 pp. Gay men and lesbians
coming out to their children.   ISBN 0-941483-44-4   9.95

LIFTING BELLY by Gertrude Stein. Ed. by Rebecca Mark. 104
pp. Erotic poetry.   ISBN 0-941483-51-7   8.95

ROSE PENSKI by Roz Perry. 192 pp. Adult lovers in a long-term
relationship.   ISBN 0-941483-37-1   8.95

AFTER THE FIRE by Jane Rule. 256 pp. Warm, human novel
by this incomparable author.   ISBN 0-941483-45-2   8.95

SUE SLATE, PRIVATE EYE by Lee Lynch. 176 pp. The gay
folk of Peacock Alley are *all cats*. ISBN 0-941483-52-5 8.95

CHRIS by Randy Salem. 224 pp. Golden oldie. Handsome Chris
and her adventures. ISBN 0-941483-42-8 8.95

THREE WOMEN by March Hastings. 232 pp. Golden oldie. A
triangle among wealthy sophisticates. ISBN 0-941483-43-6 8.95

RICE AND BEANS by Valeria Taylor. 232 pp. Love and
romance on poverty row. ISBN 0-941483-41-X 8.95

PLEASURES by Robbi Sommers. 204 pp. Unprecedented
eroticism. ISBN 0-941483-49-5 8.95

EDGEWISE by Camarin Grae. 372 pp. Spellbinding
adventure. ISBN 0-941483-19-3 9.95

FATAL REUNION by Claire McNab. 224 pp. A Carol Ashton
mystery. 2nd in a series. ISBN 0-941483-40-1 8.95

KEEP TO ME STRANGER by Sarah Aldridge. 372 pp. Romance
set in a department store dynasty. ISBN 0-941483-38-X 9.95

HEARTSCAPE by Sue Gambill. 204 pp. American lesbian in
Portugal. ISBN 0-941483-33-9 8.95

IN THE BLOOD by Lauren Wright Douglas. 252 pp. Lesbian
science fiction adventure fantasy ISBN 0-941483-22-3 8.95

THE BEE'S KISS by Shirley Verel. 216 pp. Delicate, delicious
romance. ISBN 0-941483-36-3 8.95

RAGING MOTHER MOUNTAIN by Pat Emmerson. 264 pp.
Furosa Firechild's adventures in Wonderland. ISBN 0-941483-35-5 8.95

IN EVERY PORT by Karin Kallmaker. 228 pp. Jessica's sexy,
adventuresome travels. ISBN 0-941483-37-7 9.95

OF LOVE AND GLORY by Evelyn Kennedy. 192 pp. Exciting
WWII romance. ISBN 0-941483-32-0 8.95

CLICKING STONES by Nancy Tyler Glenn. 288 pp. Love
transcending time. ISBN 0-941483-31-2 9.95

SURVIVING SISTERS by Gail Pass. 252 pp. Powerful love
story. ISBN 0-941483-16-9 8.95

SOUTH OF THE LINE by Catherine Ennis. 216 pp. Civil War
adventure. ISBN 0-941483-29-0 8.95

WOMAN PLUS WOMAN by Dolores Klaich. 300 pp. Supurb
Lesbian overview. ISBN 0-941483-28-2 9.95

HEAVY GILT by Delores Klaich. 192 pp. Lesbian detective/
disappearing homophobes/upper class gay society.

ISBN 0-941483-25-8 8.95

THE FINER GRAIN by Denise Ohio. 216 pp. Brilliant young
college lesbian novel. ISBN 0-941483-11-8 8.95

THE AMAZON TRAIL by Lee Lynch. 216 pp. Life, travel & lore
of famous lesbian author.   ISBN 0-941483-27-4   8.95

HIGH CONTRAST by Jessie Lattimore. 264 pp. Women of the
Crystal Palace.   ISBN 0-941483-17-7   8.95

OCTOBER OBSESSION by Meredith More. Josie's rich, secret
Lesbian life.   ISBN 0-941483-18-5   8.95

LESBIAN CROSSROADS by Ruth Baetz. 276 pp. Contemporary
Lesbian lives.   ISBN 0-941483-21-5   9.95

BEFORE STONEWALL: THE MAKING OF A GAY AND
LESBIAN COMMUNITY by Andrea Weiss & Greta Schiller.
96 pp., 25 illus.   ISBN 0-941483-20-7   7.95

WE WALK THE BACK OF THE TIGER by Patricia A. Murphy.
192 pp. Romantic Lesbian novel/beginning women's movement.
                                              ISBN 0-941483-13-4   8.95

SUNDAY'S CHILD by Joyce Bright. 216 pp. Lesbian athletics, at
last the novel about sports.   ISBN 0-941483-12-6   8.95

OSTEN'S BAY by Zenobia N. Vole. 204 pp. Sizzling adventure
romance set on Bonaire.   ISBN 0-941483-15-0   8.95

LESSONS IN MURDER by Claire McNab. 216 pp. A Carol
Ashton mystery. First in a series.   ISBN 0-941483-14-2   9.95

YELLOWTHROAT by Penny Hayes. 240 pp. Margarita, bandit,
kidnaps Julia.   ISBN 0-941483-10-X   8.95

SAPPHISTRY: THE BOOK OF LESBIAN SEXUALITY by
Pat Califia. 3d edition, revised. 208 pp.   ISBN 0-941483-24-X   10.95

CHERISHED LOVE by Evelyn Kennedy. 192 pp. Erotic
Lesbian love story.   ISBN 0-941483-08-8   9.95

LAST SEPTEMBER by Helen R. Hull. 208 pp. Six stories & a
glorious novella.   ISBN 0-941483-09-6   8.95

THE SECRET IN THE BIRD by Camarin Grae. 312 pp. Striking,
psychological suspense novel.   ISBN 0-941483-05-3   8.95

TO THE LIGHTNING by Catherine Ennis. 208 pp. Romantic
Lesbian 'Robinson Crusoe' adventure.   ISBN 0-941483-06-1   8.95

THE OTHER SIDE OF VENUS by Shirley Verel. 224 pp.
Luminous, romantic love story.   ISBN 0-941483-07-X   8.95

DREAMS AND SWORDS by Katherine V. Forrest. 192 pp.
Romantic, erotic, imaginative stories.   ISBN 0-941483-03-7   8.95

MEMORY BOARD by Jane Rule. 336 pp. Memorable novel
about an aging Lesbian couple.   ISBN 0-941483-02-9   9.95

THE ALWAYS ANONYMOUS BEAST by Lauren Wright
Douglas. 224 pp. A Caitlin Reece mystery. First in a series.
                                              ISBN 0-941483-04-5   8.95

SEARCHING FOR SPRING by Patricia A. Murphy. 224 pp.
Novel about the recovery of love.   ISBN 0-941483-00-2   8.95

DUSTY'S QUEEN OF HEARTS DINER by Lee Lynch. 240 pp.
Romantic blue-collar novel.   ISBN 0-941483-01-0   8.95

PARENTS MATTER by Ann Muller. 240 pp. Parents'
relationships with Lesbian daughters and gay sons.
                                                     ISBN 0-930044-91-6   9.95

THE PEARLS by Shelley Smith. 176 pp. Passion and fun in
the Caribbean sun.   ISBN 0-930044-93-2   7.95

MAGDALENA by Sarah Aldridge. 352 pp. Epic Lesbian novel
set on three continents.   ISBN 0-930044-99-1   8.95

THE BLACK AND WHITE OF IT by Ann Allen Shockley.
144 pp. Short stories.   ISBN 0-930044-96-7   7.95

SAY JESUS AND COME TO ME by Ann Allen Shockley. 288
pp. Contemporary romance.   ISBN 0-930044-98-3   8.95

LOVING HER by Ann Allen Shockley. 192 pp. Romantic love
story.   ISBN 0-930044-97-5   7.95

MURDER AT THE NIGHTWOOD BAR by Katherine V.
Forrest. 240 pp. A Kate Delafield mystery. Second in a series.
                                                     ISBN 0-930044-92-4   9.95

ZOE'S BOOK by Gail Pass. 224 pp. Passionate, obsessive love
story.   ISBN 0-930044-95-9   7.95

WINGED DANCER by Camarin Grae. 228 pp. Erotic Lesbian
adventure story.   ISBN 0-930044-88-6   8.95

PAZ by Camarin Grae. 336 pp. Romantic Lesbian adventurer
with the power to change the world.   ISBN 0-930044-89-4   8.95

SOUL SNATCHER by Camarin Grae. 224 pp. A puzzle, an
adventure, a mystery — Lesbian romance.   ISBN 0-930044-90-8   8.95

THE LOVE OF GOOD WOMEN by Isabel Miller. 224 pp.
Long-awaited new novel by the author of the beloved *Patience
and Sarah.*   ISBN 0-930044-81-9   8.95

THE HOUSE AT PELHAM FALLS by Brenda Weathers. 240
pp. Suspenseful Lesbian ghost story.   ISBN 0-930044-79-7   7.95

HOME IN YOUR HANDS by Lee Lynch. 240 pp. More stories
from the author of *Old Dyke Tales.*   ISBN 0-930044-80-0   7.95

SURPLUS by Sylvia Stevenson. 342 pp. A classic early Lesbian
novel.   ISBN 0-930044-78-9   7.95

PEMBROKE PARK by Michelle Martin. 256 pp. Derring-do
and daring romance in Regency England.   ISBN 0-930044-77-0   7.95

THE LONG TRAIL by Penny Hayes. 248 pp. Vivid adventures
of two women in love in the old west.   ISBN 0-930044-76-2   8.95